SPECIAL EDITION

WEIRDO HALLOWEEN

R.L. STINE

SCHOLASTIC INC.
New York Toronto London Auckland
Sydney Mexico City New Delhi Hong Kong

No part of this publication may be reproduced, stored in a retrieval system, or transmitted in any form or by any means, electronic, mechanical, photocopying, recording, or otherwise, without written permission of the publisher. For information regarding permission, write to Scholastic Inc., Attention: Permissions Department, 557 Broadway, New York, NY 10012.

ISBN 978-0-545-16197-8

Goosebumps book series created by Parachute Press, Inc.

Copyright © 2010 by Scholastic Inc.

All rights reserved. Published by Scholastic Inc., *Publishers since 1920.* SCHOLASTIC, GOOSEBUMPS, GOOSEBUMPS HORRORLAND, and associated logos are trademarks and/or registered trademarks of Scholastic Inc.

12 11 10 9 8 7 6 5 4 3 2 1   10 11 12 13 14 15/0

Printed in the U.S.A.   40
First printing, July 2010

MEET JONATHAN CHILLER...

He owns Chiller House, the HorrorLand gift shop. Sometimes he doesn't let kids pay for their souvenirs. Chiller tells them, "You can pay me *next time*."

What does he mean by *next time*? What is Chiller's big plan?

Go ahead — the gates are opening. Enter HorrorLand. This time you might be permitted to leave . . . but for how long? Jonathan Chiller is waiting — to make sure you TAKE A LITTLE HORROR HOME WITH YOU!

PART ONE

PART ONE

1

HorrorLand Theme Park is supposed to be "The Scariest Place on Earth." My brother, Chris, and I had to beg our parents to take us there. And then we had to beg them to let Chris and me go exploring without them.

So here we were, our first afternoon in the park — on our own — staring into the Tunnel of Screams. All I could see was a long, dark tunnel, as black as night. I could hear shrieks and muffled cries from deep inside.

"Looks awesome," I said. "Let's go." I pulled Chris into the tunnel.

We took a few steps and left the sunlight behind. In the gray light at the tunnel entrance, I could see high stone walls curving over us. Like a cave.

And flickering lights. They danced and darted along the ceiling and reminded me of the fireflies in our backyard in August. The gray light soon darkened to black as we walked farther into the tunnel.

The other kids and families weren't in sight. And all I could hear were shrill, horrifying screams. Screams that seemed to come from all sides, in front of us, behind us. Screams of terror. Long, high shrieks of fright.

"Like stepping into a horror movie," Chris said in a whisper. He was shuffling next to me, keeping close. I could barely hear him over the screams and cries.

Was I frightened? Well . . . my whole body started to tingle, and my legs felt shaky.

I guess I have to admit that I, Meg Oliver, was actually *terrified*! Maybe for the first time in my twelve years.

"Whooooooooah."

A low moan right behind me made me spin around with a gasp. But of course I couldn't see anything there.

"Chris? Where are you?" I shouted.

My brother is eleven. But sometimes he acts like a six-year-old and hides from me just to make me worry. There's only one year between us, but I'm the mature one. And the sensible one. So I'm always in charge.

"Chris?"

A shrill scream rang through the tunnel and echoed all around me.

And someone grabbed me from behind.

4

Grabbed me around the waist. And I felt hot breath on my face.

I let out a shriek — and spun around.

In the flickering firefly light, I saw Chris grinning like a cat. He let go of me and did a crazy dance.

"You creep!" I cried. I grabbed him by the ears.

Chris has giant ears. Sometimes I call him Dumbo. They are waaay too big for his head. Mom says he'll grow into them, but I don't believe it.

Sometimes when I get angry at him I grab both ears and pull with all my might. Sometimes I do it when I'm *not* angry at him. I do it just for fun. And because he hates it.

So I pulled his ears. Then I gave him a push, and we started moving again through the Tunnel of Screams.

The tunnel made a sharp turn, and we both bumped into the cold stone wall. A little girl's scream repeated and repeated, high and shrill.

Even in the dim light, I could see the fear on Chris's face. I mean, I probably looked scared, too. It's just so *frightening* to hear real people screaming in horror.

And then it got even more frightening — because I thought I recognized the screams. It sounded just like us.

"Chris —" I called. My voice trembled. "Is that *you*? Is that *you* screaming?"

I couldn't hear his reply.

And then I heard two more screams — could it be? Chris and me screaming together?

But that was impossible. Where did the screams come from?

This was HorrorLand. It had to be some kind of trick.

"Chris — are you okay? Do you hear those screams?" I cried. I grabbed for his shoulder. But I grabbed only air.

The tunnel appeared to grow darker.

"Chris? Doesn't that sound like *us*?"

No answer.

The screams were too real. I wanted the tunnel to end.

"Chris? Where are you?" I called.

Finally, squinting into the flickering light, I saw him up ahead of me. I ran and caught up. "Chris?"

I grabbed his shoulder and turned him around. And cried out in shock.

His face . . . Chris's face . . . it was GONE!

I was staring at his ugly, grinning *skull*!

2

The empty eye sockets stared up at me like deep, black tunnels. His toothless jaw moved up and down.

I stumbled back. I jerked my hand from his shoulder.

He spun away from me and ran. He quickly vanished into the darkness of the tunnel.

I blinked several times, trying to force that ugly skull from my eyes. I was panting hard. Trembling.

Finally, I caught my breath. I turned and saw that I was near the tunnel exit. Gray light seeped across the floor.

And in the weak light, I realized someone was standing in front of me. Chris! His face looked completely normal. "Meg? What's your problem? Too scared?"

"N-no," I stammered. "There was a boy. I thought he was you."

Chris crinkled his face up. "So? What's the big deal?"

"He had no face," I said. "He only had a skull. A hideous, grinning skull."

Chris laughed. "Did you forget? This is HorrorLand. Some kid was wearing a mask."

"You . . . you're probably right," I said. I started to feel a little better.

But a deep woman's voice interrupted us: "It wasn't a mask."

"Huh?" I spun around to see a large woman hovering behind us. Even in the dim light, I could see that she was strangely dressed. She wore a tall turban over her dark hair. Her pleated skirt dragged along the tunnel floor. Strings of clattering beads hung over the front of her high-necked blouse.

A long, low howl rang out through the tunnel. It sent a shiver down my back.

The woman stared from Chris to me with her glowing, dark eyes.

"It wasn't a mask," she said in her booming, deep voice. "Maybe the faceless boy revealed your future."

Chris and I gaped at her. Her perfume was spicy, like cinnamon. She had big painted lips. Her eyes didn't blink.

Chris and I both spoke at once.

"Our future?" Chris asked. "A boy with a bare skull?"

"Who are you? What do you mean?" I demanded.

"You may have heard of me," she answered. "I am Madame Doom."

Madame Doom? We'd never heard of her. We waited for her to go on.

She rattled her beaded necklaces. Then she pushed a curl of black hair up into her turban.

"Perhaps the boy without a face was a warning," she said. "Perhaps you should let me show you what life has in store for you."

"Are you some kind of fortune-teller?" I asked.

"Yes," she said. "I see the future." She motioned for us to follow her.

I felt a tingle of fear. *Maybe we should run. . . .*

I glanced at Chris. He shrugged. "Might as well," he said. "I'd like to see my future. She'll probably tell me I'll be rich and famous. Of course, I already *know* that!"

I grabbed his big ears and gave them a tug. Then we followed Madame Doom to Zombie Plaza.

Beads clattering, she led the way to a little cottage on the edge of the plaza. As we walked, I could still hear the screams pouring from the tunnel behind us.

Is that the scariest attraction at HorrorLand? I wondered. *Or will we find places even scarier?*

Curtains were drawn over the front window of the cottage. Purple light seeped through the crack between them. The doorway was also bathed in purple light.

Chris pulled me back. "You really think we should go in there?" he whispered.

"Don't be afraid," Madame Doom said. "We all have to die sometime!" She let out a booming laugh.

We followed Madame Doom into a small, cluttered front room. The air was hot inside the cottage and smelled of cinnamon, like her perfume. We had to duck under dark purple glass beads strung across the low ceiling.

Candles flickered. A glass ball about the size of a bowling ball rested on a round table. The table was cluttered with decks of cards, strange little glass figures, a stack of books. Everything glowed in the purple light.

"Take a seat," Madame Doom said softly. She pointed to two folding chairs at the table. She smiled. "That's where my victims sit."

It was a joke. But it made me feel uncomfortable. And I could see Chris blinking his eyes rapidly. He does that whenever he's really tense.

We sat down, and Madame Doom lowered her big body into the black leather chair across the table from us. The chair groaned beneath her. I heard a cat meow from behind the beaded curtain on the far wall.

"Let me see what's in your future, Meg," she said in a whisper.

A chill shot down my back. "How do you know my name?"

She didn't reply. She reached under the table and pulled something from beneath the black tablecloth.

I squinted into the purple light. She held up a doll. A rag doll. "Meg, do you believe in dark magic?"

"Huh? Dark magic?" I stared hard at it. And then a chill shook my whole body.

The doll had curly red hair, deep green eyes, and freckles on its nose. "It — it looks just like *me!*" I cried. "It — it's even wearing the same jeans and T-shirt I'm wearing now! How did you do this? *How?*"

3

I pulled the doll from Madame Doom's big hand. The stuffing inside it made a squishing sound. The hair was made with red knitting yarn. The smile was painted on.

But it was *my smile*!

"Weird," Chris said. "Let me see it, Meg."

He tried to grab it away from me, and it fell from my hand and dropped to the floor.

We both dove for it — and cracked heads.

"Owwww!" I let out a cry.

Chris handed me the doll.

I looked up — and gasped when I saw that Madame Doom was *gone*. The leather chair was empty, glowing in the purple light.

I turned to the beaded curtain. It wasn't moving. I searched all around.

"Where is she?" I cried. "How did she vanish like that?"

Chris shrugged. "Totally weird."

The doll gave me the creeps. I tossed it onto

the table and ran out the door. Chris scrambled to keep up with me. I glanced all around Zombie Plaza. No sign of her.

I guess I wasn't watching where I was going. I ran right into a tall, thin Horror and almost knocked him over.

"What's the hurry?" he groaned. He had green fur poking out from the chest of his purple overalls. He wore bright red-framed eyeglasses. A tuft of green hair stood straight up on his wide head.

The Horrors are the guides and workers at HorrorLand. They are all purple and green and very furry. They don't try to help you. They try to scare you. It's part of their job — and they seem to enjoy it!

"Have you seen Madame Doom?" Chris asked him breathlessly.

"We were just in her house," I added. I pointed to the cottage behind us.

The Horror shook his head. "Madame Doom? That's not her house," he said.

"But — but —" I stammered.

He pointed to a little glass booth across the plaza. "You want Madame Doom? There she is, over there."

"Thanks," I said.

Chris and I took off, running through the crowded plaza. We stopped in front of the booth — and gasped in shock.

13

A bright purple sign on top of the booth read: MADAME DOOM SEES ALL.

Behind a pane of glass, Madame Doom sat in the booth in front of a purple curtain. But she wasn't alive. She was a wooden dummy! A mannequin!

"That dummy — it looks just like the woman in the cottage!" Chris exclaimed.

"This has to be a joke," I murmured. I stared hard into the dummy's painted eyes. They glowed just like the living Madame Doom's eyes.

"Nothing is real in HorrorLand," Chris said. "Everyone just wants to scare you to death."

"I know, I know," I said. "But . . . who was that woman in the cottage?"

Slowly, the mannequin creaked to life. The eyes opened wider. The head nodded up and down. And then one wooden hand began to move.

Slowly, slowly, it shoved a little white card through an opening in the glass toward my brother and me.

I grabbed it and pulled it from her hand.

Would it solve the mystery?

My hand trembled. I gripped the card tightly and read it to Chris:

"'For REAL thrills and chills, you'll find your future at Chiller House! Souvenirs and Gifts!'"

Chris and I burst out laughing. "It's a crummy ad!" I cried.

"What about that woman who said she was Madame Doom?" Chris asked. "All phony, right? Do you think she works for this souvenir shop?"

"Maybe," I said. "But I can't stop thinking about that doll. It looked just like me. And it had my clothes on." I shuddered. "What do you think *that* was about?"

And then I saw the souvenir store across from us. A sign over the door read: CHILLER HOUSE.

"We have to go check it out!" Chris declared.

I took one last glance at Madame Doom. The wooden mannequin stared straight ahead, eyes blank and lifeless.

Chris and I pushed our way through the plaza

and stepped into the little shop. A bell rang over the door, but I didn't see anyone inside.

The store had two aisles of shelves and cabinets. Joke gifts and funny posters and T-shirts, magic tricks, plastic skulls, ugly creature dolls — all were piled everywhere. Hundreds of weird souvenirs and gifts.

Chris picked up a huge safety pin from the first shelf. "Check it out," he said. "The label says it's King Kong's diaper pin!"

I laughed. A brown shrunken head caught my eye. When I picked it up, water shot out of its nose. A squirting shrunken head! I squirted my brother with it. "It looks like you," I said. "Check out the huge ears."

"Ha-ha. You are so not funny!" Chris said. He poked me in the stomach with King Kong's diaper pin.

Then he put it down and picked up something else. "This is awesome!" he said. "Look. It's an abacus. Remember the abacus from first grade? Only this one is all eyeballs."

"Very cute," I said.

"Do you like the eye-bacus?" a man's voice interrupted.

We turned to see that a man had appeared at the front counter. He was big and balding. He had old-fashioned square eyeglasses perched on the end of his nose. He wore a heavy-looking brown suit with a vest, a high-collared white

16

shirt, and a bow tie. He looked a lot like the drawings of Benjamin Franklin in my history book.

"I am Jonathan Chiller," he said. "And this is my shop." When he smiled, a gold tooth gleamed in the side of his mouth.

"Cool store," Chris said. "Where do you find all this stuff?"

"From all over the universe," Chiller replied.

I picked up a stuffed two-headed monkey. Gross. I tossed it to Chris. He likes sick stuff like that.

"Look around," Chiller said. "I'm sure you'll find a good souvenir."

I pulled a strange doll down from a top shelf. It was about a foot tall, green like a grasshopper but with a fat body and a funny, froggy face.

I squeezed its smooth belly. It was made of some kind of soft rubber. When I squeezed it, the big froggy eyes popped straight out.

I laughed. "What is this weird creature?" I asked Chiller.

He came over and took it from my hand. "It's called a *Floig*," he said.

I laughed again. "Yes, it definitely looks like a Floig!" I joked.

"It's the only one I've ever seen," Chiller said. "Maybe the only one on earth."

Yeah, sure, I thought.

He handed it back to me. I squeezed its belly, and the eyes popped again.

I turned it over. It had a funny stub of a tail on its behind and rubbery little bunny feet that bent back and forth. Cute.

"I collect dolls," I told Jonathan Chiller. "Antique dolls. Not funny ones like this. But . . . it's so cute looking. I think I'll buy it."

Chiller's gold tooth gleamed as he smiled. "Good choice," he said softly.

He led the way to the front counter. He placed the Floig on its back in a long box. Then he wrapped the box with silver-and-black paper.

He tied a black ribbon around the package. Then he pulled a little doll from a drawer. It was a tiny green-and-purple Horror. Like the park guides.

Chiller attached the little doll to the ribbon. He smiled at me again. "Take a little Horror home with you," he said.

He handed me the box.

I reached into my backpack for my money. "How much do I owe you?" I asked.

Chiller waved me away. "Don't pay me now," he said. "You can pay me back the next time you see me."

Next time?

What did he mean by *that*?

PART TWO

PART TWO

5

We drove home the next day. But we had a surprise in store for us. In the car, Mom and Dad said they had to go to Chicago on a business trip.

"I can't believe you won't be home for Halloween," I said. "It's this weekend. Who is going to decorate the house?"

"You and Chris can decorate," Dad said. "You know where I keep the orange lights, and the skulls, and the plastic jack-o'-lanterns."

Chris shook his head and slumped down in the backseat. "It won't be the same. Who's coming to stay with us?"

"Penny," Mom said.

"Huh? Penny? You're joking!" Chris and I cried together.

"Don't act so surprised. She's known you since you were babies," Mom said.

"But she's a hundred and twenty!" Chris cried.

Dad laughed. "She's not that old. She's only a

hundred and eighteen. And she has the energy of a hundred-and-ten-year-old!"

That made Chris and me laugh. Penny is our old babysitter. She used to live with us until we really didn't need a full-time babysitter anymore. She's tiny and frail, like a little sparrow. And she has terrible eyesight.

Chris and I always loved her because she's a total flake. And she let us do whatever we wanted — because she couldn't really see what we were doing!

We were a few miles from home when my friend Kelly texted me. She was reminding Chris and me not to forget her Halloween party tomorrow night. Kelly always likes to be early. Her party was the day before Halloween!

She asked how HorrorLand was.

"Horrifying," I texted back. And I meant it.

I couldn't wait to get home. I wanted to get to work on my vampire costume for Kelly's party.

Kelly loves to do fashion drawings. She's always filling up her notebook with sketches of models in crazy outfits. She's really talented. I didn't want my costume to be totally embarrassing next to hers.

I poked Chris in the side. He pulled his iPod earbuds from his ears. "Do you have a costume for Kelly's party?" I asked.

He snickered. "I bought these pointy ears. I'm going to put them on and go as a Vulcan from *Star Trek*."

"That's totally dumb," I said.

"I know," he replied. He shoved the earbuds back into his ears. His head bobbed up and down to the music.

"You look like a bobblehead doll," I said.

He didn't hear me.

At home, I unpacked quickly. I unwrapped the Floig and gazed at it. It stared back at me with its big, black froggy eyes. I squeezed its soft green belly.

"Where am I going to put you?" I murmured.

My antique doll collection takes up nearly one whole wall in my room. I have some wonderful dolls from the 1920s and 1930s. They have life-like hair in old-fashioned styles and very sweet and pretty faces.

My oldest doll is from the 1890s. I call her Elizabeth. She belonged to my great-great-grandmother.

The doll has beautiful blond braided hair. Her long pink skirt is in pretty good shape. But the color on her face is totally washed out.

I don't care. Elizabeth is my favorite doll. Mainly because she's been in our family for so long.

I squeezed the Floig again. It felt good. Like a soft beanbag.

Then I placed it in the corner of my desk. I picked up the little Horror that Jonathan Chiller had attached to the wrapping. And I placed it next to the Floig.

I had to laugh. The Floig looked so ugly compared to all my beautiful old dolls, I just couldn't put them near each other.

I had no way of knowing that the funny-looking thing would save my life.

My parents left the next morning. Penny arrived when Chris and I got home from school that afternoon.

She stepped into the house, squinting through her thick eyeglasses and carrying a round gold-fish bowl in both hands.

Chris and I were happy to see her. We both ran to give her hugs. But she held the fishbowl up in front of her.

"The yellowish one is Arlo," she said. "The one in the middle is Jeffrey. And the pretty one? I named her Meg, after you."

"Oh, that's so nice!" I gushed. I peered into the water. The three bobbing goldfish looked exactly alike. "Which one is Meg?" I asked.

"The pretty one," Penny replied. She set the bowl down on the coffee table. Her bones made kind of a creaking sound as she bent over.

She straightened up and spread out her arms

for hugs. She was so tiny, almost like a stick figure. I tried not to hug her too hard.

Her short hair was bright orange. She had a small black-and-orange pumpkin clip on one side. Her lips were orange to match her hair. She smelled like lemons.

"I want to hear everything you've been doing," she said. She lowered herself into the armchair beside the coffee table and took out her knitting. "Calm down, Arlo," she said, squinting at the fishbowl. "You're making Jeffrey and Meg nervous."

"We just got back from HorrorLand," Chris told her.

"I heard that's a scary place," Penny said. "Did you see any ghosts?"

"Not really," Chris said.

"My house in New Hampshire was haunted," Penny said. "You know, ghosts won't hurt you unless you stare them in the eye."

I squinted at the pile of knitting in her lap. "Penny, what are you making?"

"It's a sweater," she said. "For my nephew." She held it up.

Chris and I exchanged glances. We both saw that the sweater had *three arms*. Penny had worse eyesight than we thought!

"Maybe her nephew has three arms," Chris whispered.

I held a finger up to my lips. "Don't embarrass her."

"My fish like Halloween," Penny said. "I give them special treats."

"Sweet!" I said. I told her about the Halloween party at Kelly's house.

"Don't stay out too late," Penny said. "I go to bed at seven-thirty. But I'll leave all the lights on."

At seven-thirty, we said good night to Penny. Then we headed outside to walk to Kelly's house.

I stopped on the front walk and did a slow twirl. My cape swirled around me. "Well?" I gave Chris a shove. "You didn't say anything about my costume. What do you think?"

"Awesome," he said. He barely looked at it. "What are you supposed to be? A gypsy?"

"No, you idiot!" I shoved him away. "See the fangs? The black lipstick? I'm a vampire! I spent *hours* on this costume. Look. I even dyed my hair black."

"Meg, you look much better as a vampire," he said, grinning. "Are you going to bite someone's neck?"

I rolled my eyes. "Ha-ha." I walked faster, trying to get away from him.

"I know whose neck you're going to bite," Chris said, jogging to catch up to me. "Justin

27

Goldberg. You're going to bite his neck — *aren't* you, Meg?"

I spun around angrily. "Have you totally lost your mind? No *way* I'd bite Justin Goldberg's neck."

"You would," Chris insisted. "Because he's your boyfriend. You'd love to turn him into your vampire slave."

I let out a cry. I tried to shove Chris, but he danced out of the way. "Someone should lock you up," I said. "You're totally whacked or something!"

I made a grab for his pointy ears. I wanted to rip them off and throw them into the street. But my arms got tangled in my cape, and I had to stop and untangle myself.

I shivered. It was a cold night for October. The ground was crunchy and hard from the frost. A thin sliver of a moon, like a fingernail clipping, hung low in the black sky.

"I don't even *like* Justin Goldberg!" I shouted. Chris was dancing on the sidewalk, walking backward, up ahead of me. "So don't make up stuff about me!"

He started to laugh. But then his eyes went wide and he stopped dancing. "Meg?" he cried in a soft whisper. He pointed to the hedges beside the walk.

I trotted up to him and followed his gaze.

"I see it!" I whispered.

We were both staring at something in the hedge. It was alive! Something caught in its brambles. Squirming frantically.

I took a step closer. And pressed my hands against my cheeks.

"Oh, no!" I cried. "It's . . . it's a BABY!"

"It's *not* a baby!" I cried. "Too big!"

But what *was* it?

I crept up to the hedge, breathing hard.

What could it be? We took a closer look. It looked like a small boy — with orange skin. He wore a blue T-shirt over a big diaper. He was kicking his legs frantically. I saw shiny red shoes on his feet.

He thrashed his skinny arms. He was grunting in a funny hoarse voice.

"Hold still," I said. "We'll get you out."

But he kept kicking those little red shoes and grunting and twisting.

I reached both hands into the hedge and wrapped them around his middle. Then I gave a hard tug — and he popped right out.

I uttered a startled cry. I couldn't believe how *light* he was. Like he weighed about ten pounds!

I was so surprised, I nearly dropped him.

But I managed to set him down on his red shoes. He kept making those grunting sounds and flapping his little arms, like he was still stuck in the hedge.

Chris and I stared at him. Was he a boy dressed as a baby? What a weird Halloween costume! A T-shirt and a diaper? That orange skin?

But wait. He had two slender antennae on top of his bald head. Like snail antennae.

Was he supposed to be an *alien* baby? A mutant?

He finally stopped grunting. He raised his face to us. He had tiny black eyes. They looked like raisins.

"Are you okay?" I asked. "How did you get caught in that hedge?"

He didn't answer.

"Cool costume," Chris said. "Did you buy it, or did you make it?"

No answer. He gazed up at us with those little eyes. His mouth moved silently up and down.

"Do you live around here?" I asked. "I'm Meg Oliver. He's my brother, Chris. We live in that house on the next block." I pointed.

"Are you hurt?" Chris asked.

"No." The boy finally spoke. He had a strange tinny voice. "My feeling is okay."

Chris and I glanced at each other. We were both thinking the same thing: Why did he have such a weird voice? It was like a cartoon character.

"Are you sure you're okay?" I asked.

He nodded. "My feeling is okay." He hugged himself. He must have been freezing in that costume!

"How old are you?" Chris asked.

"Many," the kid replied. He held up one hand. He had only *three* fingers!

"How did you do that?" I asked. "Is it a special glove?"

"Are you dressed as an alien baby?" Chris asked him.

He tossed back his head and opened his mouth in a tinny laugh. He sounded a lot like SpongeBob!

A cold gust of wind made me shudder. I wrapped my black cape around me.

"You're putting us on, right?" I said. "You're doing that funny voice?"

"My feeling is funny," he replied. His smile was all crooked on his orange face. He laughed again, raising his eyes to the black sky.

"Do you go to our school?" Chris asked.

The kid stared back at him but didn't reply.

"We're going to be late," I told Chris. "I promised Kelly I'd get there early."

"Yeah. Well, awesome costume," Chris told the kid.

"Bye," I said. "Stay out of the hedges."

Chris and I turned and walked away. The wind was swirling around us. A cloud rolled over the tiny sliver of moon, and the street grew darker.

Chris and I started to trot. Kelly's house was the last one on the block, across from Becker Woods. My cape fluttered behind me as we hurried. I knew my hair was a mess.

Kelly had all the lights on. A huge, fiery jack-o'-lantern grinned at us on the front stoop. Chris and I leaped onto the stoop. I rang the doorbell.

I heard a sound behind us. I turned. "Oh, I don't believe it," I whispered.

Chris turned to see what I saw. The orange kid in the diaper had followed us. He stood staring at us from the sidewalk.

Kelly's front door swung open. I heard a growl.

I jumped to the side as Kelly's big dog came roaring out, barking ferociously.

"Noooooo!" A scream burst from my throat as the dog lowered his head and leaped off the stoop. In a frenzy of growls and snapping teeth, he tore straight at the little kid.

8

I screamed again.

To my shock, the dog stopped short. He pulled back a few inches from the kid. It was like he'd hit an invisible wall.

The dog lowered his head. He tucked his tail between his hind legs and began to whimper. His whole body trembled.

The kid hadn't moved. He had his hands at his waist. His tiny raisin eyes were trained on the trembling dog.

Kelly burst onto the stoop. "What did you do to Bubba?" she cried. She pointed. "Look at him. He's shaking like a leaf!"

"He . . . he jumped at that kid," I stammered.

Kelly blinked. "Kid? What kid?"

I turned back. The little orange guy had vanished.

Kelly leaped off the stoop and threw her arms around Bubba's neck. "Are you okay, baby? You hate Halloween, don't you?"

"There was a little kid standing there in a weird costume," Chris said. "I guess the kid scared him."

"Dogs hate Halloween," Kelly said. "It's just too weird for them. They don't get it at all."

She gave Bubba a final pat on the head. The dog was still trembling. He slowly climbed up the stoop and walked back into the house.

I heard kids laughing inside. And loud music.

"I was going to make Bubba a costume," she said. "You know. For the party. But I knew he'd just tear it apart and eat it."

"He's always so gentle," I said. "It's weird that he wanted to attack that kid."

I realized Kelly was staring hard at me. I suddenly knew why.

I burst out laughing. "Kelly — I don't believe it! Your costume is almost identical to mine!"

She threw an arm around my shoulders, and we both laughed. Our capes got tangled together.

"Meg, we've been best friends so long," she said. "We even think of the same Halloween costume!"

"Your makeup is better," I said. "Your eyes really look like they're sunken deep in your head. And your blue lips are awesome."

"Your black lipstick is better," Kelly said. "Much creepier."

"I think *my* costume is the best," Chris chimed in.

We ignored him. We bumped him out of the way and walked into the party.

Kelly's living room was hot and already crowded. I stepped under orange and black streamers strung over the ceiling. I saw a grinning skull on the coffee table, surrounded by huge black plastic spiders. Black candles flickered everywhere.

Eerie music boomed from the stereo. Everyone was in costume. I saw a ghost in a bedsheet. I saw two mummies at the food table, trying to pick up tortilla chips with their bandaged hands. A pirate with a black eye patch and a parrot on his shoulder waved to Chris. Probably one of my brother's buddies.

"Did you see Melody?" Kelly asked. "She's a riot. She's dressed as a mushroom. Really."

I glanced around. No sign of a mushroom.

I turned toward the den, and a tall two-headed alien stepped in front of me.

"Hi, Carlos," I said.

Silence for a moment. Then his voice seemed to come from far away. "Meg, how'd you know it was me?"

I rolled my eyes. "You're the only science-fiction geek I know," I said. "Who *else* would come here in a two-headed alien costume?"

Both of his heads stared at me. One head was

bright blue and had a nose that stuck straight out like a bumpy cucumber. The other head was red and had four eyes, two noses, and two mouths with dripping fangs.

"Can you tell which is my real head?" Carlos asked.

"They both are!" I joked.

He didn't laugh. "No. Take a guess. Which mask is my head in?"

His voice was so muffled, I could barely hear him over the loud voices and creepy music.

I gazed at the blue head, then the red head.

"Neither one," Carlos answered before I could guess. "My real head is buried inside the chest of this costume."

I laughed. "Totally clever."

"There's only one problem," Carlos said. "I can't see a thing. Where am I? Who am I talking to?"

Carlos is the funniest dude I know. He's a good friend.

And he knows everything about aliens and mutants and every sci-fi movie ever made. He spends all his time online reading strange blogs. He's totally into it.

He stepped past me to show off his costume to some kids who had just arrived. I turned and saw Bubba. The poor thing was huddled in a corner, head down, still shaking.

What was *that* about?

Kelly's Halloween party was awesome. Her mom kept bringing in more and more pizzas. We played a scary hide-and-seek game across the street in Becker Woods.

Then we came back to the house to warm up. After we drank hot apple cider, Kelly turned off all the lights. We sat around the living room, gazing into the flickering flames of the black candles.

Carlos pulled off his two heads and set them down on the floor. He leaned into the dancing candlelight and told a scary ghost story. "This is the story of the headless ghost," he said in a whisper.

A hush fell over the room. I had to struggle to hear his whispered story over the gusting wind outside the living room window.

"You may not believe in ghosts," Carlos said. "But Kelly does — because the headless ghost lives in her basement."

Kelly laughed, breaking the silence.

"Kelly always laughs to cover up the truth," Carlos whispered. "She doesn't want anyone to know of the hideous ghost that haunts her house. She doesn't want anyone to know why she removed the ghost's head. She'll never tell where she hid that ugly head."

"Carlos, it's on your neck!" someone shouted.

Everyone laughed.

"It's easy to make jokes," Carlos whispered. "When you're afraid. And we all have a reason to be afraid. Because if you listen carefully . . . No one make a sound. Just listen. And you will hear the headless ghost coming up the basement stairs. You will hear the creak of its footsteps. Listen . . ."

The room grew silent again. No one moved. We were all listening.

I felt a chill at the back of my neck.

I screamed when a deafening crash shattered the silence.

Sharp pieces of glass shot over the room. Other kids screamed. Some dove to the floor.

A rush of freezing wind blew over us. Blew out all the candles.

Darkness now — and the clatter of glass — and the steady rush of wind.

I stumbled up from the couch arm where I'd been sitting. I staggered a few steps in the darkness.

Kids were shouting and crying out startled questions:

"What happened?"

"What crashed?"

"Did something blow up?"

"Was that broken glass?"

For a brief second, I thought of Carlos's headless ghost. He told us to listen for it — and then . . .

A crazy thought.

Someone clicked the ceiling lights back on. I gazed around. Everyone looked so stunned, so confused. Kids climbed to their feet, shaking their heads.

"It's the window!" Kelly yelled.

I turned. Yes. The living room window had been shattered. I saw a big jagged hole in the center with cracks zigzagging over the rest of the pane.

Kelly started for the window, then stopped. She knelt down beside a brown package on the carpet in front of the broken window.

"Hey — did someone toss this through the window?" she said.

Crunching over broken glass, kids gathered around the package.

"What is it?" I cried. "Kelly — be careful! Don't open it."

I hurried up beside her. My warning was too late.

She was already tearing it open.

"Who would do this?" she cried. Her hands were trembling as she ripped at the package. "Who would heave something through my living room window?"

She tore off the lid — and *whooooosh*!

I felt a blast of hot air against my face.

I raised my hands to shield myself. I stumbled back a few steps into Carlos. He caught me and stood me up straight.

And then the horrible odor invaded my nose.

"Ohhhhhh." I let out a sickened moan.

I saw other kids' eyes go wide. Their mouths twisted in disgust.

And Kelly shrieked at the top of her lungs:

"Oh, help! Help! What's that *disgusting* smell?"

10

I tried to hold my breath. But it was too late. The sour smell was already in my nose and mouth.

I squeezed two fingers over my nose. My stomach lurched. I struggled to keep the pizza down.

The room rang with the sick moans and cries of all the kids. Still holding my breath, I spun around and searched for my brother. But my eyes began pouring out tears. I could barely see.

Finally, I found Chris, bending over the couch, struggling not to puke.

My stomach heaved again. I couldn't help it. I had to take a breath. And I got another sharp mouthful of the bitter, disgusting odor.

I started to gag. I stumbled toward Chris at the couch. And bumped hard into Melody.

She struggled to pull off her mushroom costume. She was choking and gagging, stumbling toward the front door.

I heard the door crash against the wall as it was pulled open. Kids were running out of the house, moaning and retching. The living room carpet was littered with costumes and masks.

In one corner, I saw Bubba, Kelly's dog, with his head lowered, tail between his legs. His whole body was shuddering.

Kelly was sprawled on the floor. She looked dazed. She was panting hard.

Holding my breath, my chest aching, I stumbled over to her. "Kelly? Are you okay?"

She shook her head no.

"Can you breathe?" I asked.

"I . . . I guess," she choked out.

All around us, kids screamed and cried and moaned. They stampeded out the door. The room was nearly empty.

Chris staggered up to us. One of his pointy ears had fallen off.

"Whoa. That smelled like a dead horse!" he cried. He picked up the brown package from beside Kelly on the floor. "What is this? Some kind of powerful stink bomb?"

"Put it down!" I cried. "Maybe it has more inside it."

He tossed it across the room.

"Who . . .?" Kelly moaned. "Who would . . .?" Swallowing hard, she gazed at the broken front window.

43

I patted her shoulder. "Take a deep breath," I said. "The smell is almost gone. Try to calm down."

"Who . . .?" she repeated. "Meg, who would do that? Who would throw a disgusting stink bomb through my living room window?"

I shook my head. I didn't know what to say.

"Who hates me that much?" she cried. Tears rolled down her red, swollen face. "Who hates me that much to ruin my party and wreck my house? Who?"

"I don't know," I said softly. I grabbed her by the arms and helped her to her feet. "I don't know anyone who would do such a horrible thing."

Kelly rocked back. I held her steady till she caught her balance.

"Man, that thing totally *stunk*!" Chris exclaimed. He turned to Kelly. "And you got the major blast."

"I . . . I can still smell it," Kelly said in a trembling voice. "It's on my skin! On my clothes!"

I wiped tears off her cheeks with my fingers. "Chris and I will help you clean up," I said.

"We will?" Chris said.

I gave him a playful karate chop in the stomach. "Yes, we will."

Behind us, Bubba groaned and lay down on the floor.

I turned to Kelly. "Where are your parents?"

44

Kelly shook her head. "They thought the party was under control. So they went to a late movie." She let out a long sigh. "Look at this room. The window . . . When they get home, they're going to *kill* me!"

"We can clean up most of it," I said. I kicked a sharp triangle of glass out of my way. "First, let's wipe up the puke. Where are the paper towels? We need rolls and rolls of paper towels."

The three of us started to work. We didn't say a word. The eerie music was still playing. Kelly shut it off with a sob. She kept shaking her head and muttering to herself.

My stomach felt shaky. Cleaning up puke isn't my favorite job. I scrubbed really hard. But there were orange and yellow stains all over the carpet and furniture.

"Do you have air freshener?" I asked Kelly.

That question made her start to cry again. Her black eye makeup ran down the sides of her face.

"We need a *ton* of air freshener!" Chris said, holding his nose.

"Shut up," I said. "That's not helpful."

He crunched over a shard of glass. "How about if I get the vacuum cleaner?" he said. "If we get rid of the broken glass, the room will almost be back to normal."

"No, it won't," Kelly murmured. "Nothing will ever be normal again."

I couldn't blame her for being so upset. She had been throwing the best Halloween party in history, and someone deliberately ruined it.

Who could it have been? Someone she forgot to invite? Just about every kid in our class was there.

My brain spun. I couldn't think of anyone who hated Kelly or had a grudge against her. I couldn't think of anyone who would play such a mean and harmful joke.

The three of us vacuumed and cleaned the carpet. We did the best we could.

I told Kelly I'd call her in the morning. Then Chris and I started for home.

As we walked, we both struggled to think of who might have ruined Kelly's party. But we couldn't come up with a single name.

Chris sniffed hard two or three times. "I can still smell that stink on my clothes," he murmured. "Wonder if it'll ever come out."

The cold wind swirled around us. We were shivering by the time we got home.

We went in through the back door. Penny was asleep, but she left all the lights on for us.

We climbed the stairs. I stepped into my bedroom.

And let out a cry.

The orange baby-kid stood in front of my dresser. "Did you get the message?" he asked.

11

Chris heard my scream and came running into my room. We both stared at the kid in the weird costume.

His baggy blue T-shirt came down over his diaper. He leaned on the dresser and tapped one red shoe on the floor.

"My feeling is lonely," he said in his tinny cartoon voice. "I sent you aroma message. To come home."

"Huh?" I cried. "*What* did you send us?"

"Aroma message," the kid repeated.

I nearly choked. I took two or three steps toward him. "*You* did that?" I shouted angrily. "You threw a stink bomb through Kelly's window?"

He nodded his round head. He had a big grin on his face. Like he was proud of what he did.

"How COULD you?" I screamed. "Your aroma message ruined my friend's party. And it made a lot of kids sick."

47

The kid's grin stayed plastered on his face. "You got message," he said.

"Who *are* you?" Chris demanded. "How did you get in our house?"

"Never mind," I said. "Just get *out* of here. Really. I mean it. Get out!"

"But my feeling is lonely," the kid said.

Why did he talk so strange in that weird hoarse voice? It had to be a joke. But the joke wasn't very funny.

"My name Bim," he said. The orange antennae on top of his head wiggled as he talked. "You know my planet? Weirdo Planet?"

I rolled my eyes. "Okay, sure," I said. "You're a weirdo. Very funny. You can go home now." I motioned to the door.

"You're a little *too* weird," Chris said. "Go home, dude!"

"No. Bim is home," the kid said. His raisin eyes glowed darkly. "First time on your planet. Bim never visit before."

I turned to Chris. "Should we call 911?" I whispered. "Call the police?"

Chris shrugged. "Beats me. This kid is a nut job."

Bim picked up a glass paperweight from my dresser top and began rolling it between his three-fingered hands. He smiled again. "You saved Bim's life."

I squinted at him. "Excuse me?"

"You mean because we pulled you from that hedge?" Chris asked.

Bim nodded. "Yes. Bim's life saved by you. So my feeling is happy."

"Big thrill," I said. "Will you please go home now?"

"Bim *is* home," he replied. "You save Bim's life. Bim belongs to you now."

My mouth dropped open.

What kind of dumb joke was this kid pulling?

He licked the glass paperweight with a fat pink tongue. Licked it all around. Then set it back on my dresser.

"It's really late," I said. "Why don't you give us a break?"

His antennae stood straight up. "Translate, please."

"Just go home!" Chris said through clenched teeth. He balled his hands into tight fists. I could see my brother was about to lose it.

"This my home now," the weirdo repeated. "I belong to you now. You save Bim's life."

"Are you *crazy*?" I screamed. "We didn't save your life. We just pulled you out of a hedge!"

Chris turned to me. "Is this kid for *real*?"

I felt a shiver run down my back. I suddenly pictured Bubba, Kelly's dog. At first, Bubba came bursting out of the house to attack this kid. But the dog stopped suddenly and started to shake with fright.

Something very strange was happening here. Strange and frightening. I began to believe this *wasn't* a kid in a funny costume.

But what *was* he?

Is he dangerous? I wondered.

"My feeling is happy," the kid said. He did a little dance, tapping his shiny red shoes on the floor.

"You're going to wake up Penny," I said. "Please . . . please . . . I'm begging you to leave."

"Where Bim sleep?" he asked, gazing around.

"You sleep at your own house," Chris said. "You know, dude, this joke isn't funny anymore. It's just stupid."

Once again, Bim's snail-like antennae stood straight up. "Translate, please," he said.

"I'll translate," Chris shouted. "It means I'm kicking your butt out of here!"

He dove forward and grabbed the little kid around the neck. Then he slid his hands under the kid's armpits. And hoisted him into the air.

"Oh, NO!" Chris let out a startled cry — as Bim flew from his hands and went sailing up to the ceiling.

CRAAASSSHH.

He smacked the ceiling hard.

"Chris — you've hurt him! You've *hurt* him!" I cried.

12

"WHEEEEE!" Bim cried. "Ceiling game fun. Do again! Do again!"

He came floating down slowly. I moved under him and caught him in my arms. "He — really is light as a feather!" I cried.

Chris was breathing hard. "That's why he got away from me," he said.

"Let Bim down," the kid said in his funny voice. "Bim live here now."

"No, you don't," I said. I held him tightly and started for the door. "You're leaving now, Bim — or whatever your real name is."

"It's so weird," Chris said, following me to the bedroom door. "He weighs less than Aunt Lucy's Chihuahua! Maybe he's telling the truth, Meg. Maybe —"

I was nearly into the hall when Bim started to change. He shut his tiny eyes tight and clenched his whole face. He began to grit his teeth. Then

51

disgusting grunting sounds came up from his throat.

"Rrrrruggggh. Rrrrrrugggggh."

I gasped as he began to feel heavier. I struggled to hold him up.

But he was gaining weight fast.

"Ohhh!" I tried to grab on tighter. But he was too heavy.

Pain shot down my back and arms. I had to drop him to the floor.

He landed with a hard, loud thud.

"He — he weighs a thousand pounds!" I stammered.

Bim crossed his arms in front of his slender chest and glared at us. His face was bright orange now.

"How did you do that?" I screamed. My voice came out high and shrill. "What's going on here? You're not really an alien from outer space! You *can't* be!"

I totally lost it. I reached down to his chin and grabbed the bottom of his mask. "Let's see who you *really* are!"

13

I tugged on the kid's mask.

I tugged harder.

I gasped. Then I jerked my hand back and nearly stumbled into my brother.

"It's NOT a mask!" I choked out. "That's his real face."

Chris's eyes went wide. "For real?"

"For real."

I stared at the orange guy, about three feet tall with his baby face and perky antennae . . . his three-fingered hands . . . those raisin eyes.

All real. Not a Halloween costume.

A cold wave of panic ran down my back.

Bim didn't move. He just stood there, glaring at Chris and me with his arms crossed.

"T-tell us the truth," I stammered. "Who are you?"

"Bim," he replied. "Bim Bim Bim. My name Bim. I am Weirdo."

Chris took a step back. His voice shook with fear. "But . . . how did you get here?" he asked. "Why did you land in our neighborhood?"

"Why I land here?" Bim replied. He rubbed his round orange chin. "I try remember."

Then he stopped. He made a hoarse coughing noise. Then he cleared his throat really loud.

"Excuse Bim," he said.

He opened his mouth wide . . . wider. He began to cough and sputter. He made raspy choking noises from deep in his throat.

Then, with a *SPLUTTTT*, something wet and disgusting slid out of his open mouth — and plopped onto my bedspread.

"Oh, *sick!*" Chris groaned. "It's some kind of dead animal, covered in yellow slime!"

"Excuse Bim," he said, wiping the wet mucus off his lips with the back of one hand. He spit a fat glob of yellow mucus onto the floor.

I blinked several times and gaped at the sticky mess on my bed. A dead bird. Still whole. Its feathers matted to its body by yellow slime.

My stomach heaved. I pressed a hand over my mouth.

I heard a sound at the door.

I spun around and saw Penny come shuffling into the room. She squinted through her thick glasses at the dead bird on my bedspread. Her eyes bulged and she let out a cry:

"Meg! What's THAT?"

54

My heart skipped a beat.

Penny leaned over the bed and squinted at the yucky dead bird on the bedspread.

Think fast, Meg! I told myself.

Chris and I didn't want to upset our old babysitter. She was so frail and weak.

But how could I explain a whole mucus-covered dead bird on my bed?

"It . . . it's a Halloween thing," I told Penny. "A joke. You know. It's made out of rubber or something."

Penny turned and lowered her gaze on Bim.

"That's our friend . . . Max," Chris told her. "Isn't that an awesome baby costume?"

"Everyone loved Max's costume at Kelly's party," I added.

I hated to be such a liar. But it was for Penny's own good.

Penny laughed. "That's wonderful," she told Bim. "Very clever. Did you make it yourself?"

"Bim made it," he answered, nodding his head.

Penny wrinkled her face. "Bim?"

"That's his brother's name," I said. "His brother is an art student. He is always making interesting things."

Penny nodded. "Nice to meet you, Max." She turned to me. "I got up to give my fish their late feeding. They always enjoy a midnight snack."

We watched her leave the room. She walked with slow, shuffling steps.

We listened to her pad down the stairs. Then Chris and I turned back to Bim.

"Close call," I said with a sigh.

Bim picked the slimy dead bird off the bedspread in one three-fingered hand. He pushed it into my face. "Taste?"

It smelled worse than a skunk! "*Uggggh*. No way!" I cried, backing away.

He held the dead bird by a leg and swung it under Chris's nose. "Taste?"

Chris shook his head. His whole body shuddered. "I . . . I don't think so."

Bim shoved the bird back into his mouth. He swallowed it whole. It made a *ssssllllliiiccck* sound as it slid down his throat. Then he wiped sticky stuff off his cheeks and lips.

"Bim eat only *living* meat," he explained. "Living meat taste fresh."

My stomach heaved again. I felt totally nauseous.

"Bim heave up food three times before food stay down," the alien continued.

I stared at him. He still had some yellow slime on his chin. "You mean every time you eat, you have to puke three times?" I asked.

He nodded. "My feeling is happy. That was third time. Tasting so good."

I turned to Chris. "I'm going to be sick. Really."

"Not sick. My feeling is happy," Bim said. "You nice new owners. Bim stay with you forever."

I swallowed hard, waiting for my stomach to settle.

"What if we say *please*," Chris said to Bim. "What if we say *pretty-please. Then* would you leave?"

"Yes," I said. "Please. Please. Bim, we are begging you. Please leave our house."

His antennae stood straight up. He raised one hand. "Bim swear will be loyal slave. Bim swear never leave you."

"But . . . we're *begging* you!" I cried. "Don't you understand? We *want* you to go away!"

His antennae drooped. He lowered his hand to his side. He narrowed his tiny eyes and scrunched up his face until it wrinkled like an orange prune.

"Don't make my feeling *unhappy*!" he growled.

I gasped.

Was that a threat?

The little guy suddenly looked menacing.

His eyes grew bold and blacker. His lips pulled back, and I saw *three* rows of pointed teeth! Slowly, the teeth began to grind.

And then as I stared, frozen in horror, straight yellow fangs slid down over his bottom lip. He began to pant like an animal, sucking drool on his fangs.

Chris and I both backed up.

Thick white foam spread over Bim's open mouth. He snarled, and his fangs slid lower, down over his chin. He raised himself on tiptoe.

He didn't look like a cute baby any longer. His face darkened to red. His chest swelled under the blue shirt.

He leaned toward us, eyes spinning wildly in his head.

And then he opened his mouth in a bellowing roar: "DON'T MAKE MY FEELING *UNHAPPY*!"

14

My heart was doing flip-flops in my chest. Staring at this ... this MONSTER, my whole body began to shake.

"Okay, okay," I choked out. I backed up until I bumped into my dresser.

Chris's mouth hung open in fright. He leaped aside as the angry alien lurched forward.

The white foam bubbled from Bim's mouth. His fangs made a scraping sound as they rubbed his chin. His face darkened to purple. "Don't make my feeling unhappy," he growled again.

How dangerous was this alien? Would he really hurt Chris and me?

Living meat.

He said he ate only living meat. Did that include *humans*?

Could he swallow us whole like that poor dead bird? And then puke us up two or three times?

I knew I had to calm him down. "Listen ...
Bim..." I started. "Chris and I would *love* for
you to stay. Really."

He stopped grunting and frothing. His face
brightened back to tomato red.

"But there's just nowhere for you to sleep," I
continued. "See?" I waved around my room.
"There's no place for you."

"She's right," Chris chimed in. "There's just
no room, Bim."

Bim stared hard at Chris, then at me. He
gnashed his teeth loudly. White foam drooled
onto my rug.

"My feeling *very* unhappy," Bim rasped.
"Never make Bim's feeling unhappy. Because ...
see what happens."

He spun around, turning his back on us. He
walked heavily up to my wall of shelves. And
he grabbed a doll off the middle shelf.

"No!" I screamed. "What are you going to do?"

Bim raised the doll in front of him. He held it
up so I could see it clearly.

"No — please!" I cried. "Put her down!
She's my oldest doll. That's Elizabeth. She
belonged to my great-great-grandmother! Put
her down, Bim!"

Bim lowered the doll.

"She's my most valuable doll. Put her down.
That's right," I said in a trembling voice.
"Down ... down ..."

Bim lowered the doll to the shelf. Then he picked up the one next to it. One of my favorites, from the 1930s.

"Bim, please —"

He ignored me. He lowered the doll to his drooling mouth. Then he shoved the doll's head into his mouth — and bit it off.

It made a sick *craaaack*.

I screamed.

He spit the head out. It hit the carpet and rolled halfway across the room.

"Bim, please —" I begged again.

He ignored me. His eyes whirled crazily as he began to spin the headless doll between his teeth. He spun it faster . . . faster. Like the lathe we have in the wood shop at school.

It made a whirring, grinding sound as he spun the doll between his teeth. In a few seconds, I stared at a pile of wood shavings on the floor.

My doll. One of my most precious dolls. Chewed to bits.

Bim shook the shavings off his red shoes. He spit out a splinter.

I was trembling all over. I turned to Chris with tears in my eyes.

"He's really dangerous," I whispered. "What are we going to do?"

15

"We'd better keep him happy," Chris whispered. "Until we can figure out a way to get rid of him."

"Should we tell Penny?" I asked.

"No," Chris said. "We don't want to upset her. She's so frail. Besides, there's no way she could help. . . ."

I stared at Bim. He was breathing hard, sucking his fangs noisily, still red in the face.

I took a deep breath. "I . . . want to keep you feeling happy," I said.

He instantly relaxed. His fangs slid up into his gums. His skin faded to orange. His antennae wiggled on top of his head.

"You want make Bim feeling happy?" he asked softly.

I nodded. "Yes. What can I do?"

"You rub my back," he said. He plopped down on the carpet. He sat cross-legged and tugged off the blue T-shirt. "Rub Bim's back for hour, maybe two."

I didn't know what to do. I glanced at Chris. He shrugged.

"Uh . . . I don't think so," I said.

Bim turned and picked up another doll from the shelf. Elizabeth!

He raised her to his mouth.

"Okay, okay!" I cried. "I'll rub your back."

He lowered Elizabeth to the shelf.

I stepped up behind him. I gazed down at his shiny orange skin. This was creepy. I didn't really want to touch him.

"Rub Bim's back," he repeated. He rolled his bony shoulders.

I lowered my hands to his shoulders.

Ohhh, yuck.

His skin felt disgusting. Damp and hot and lumpy. Kind of like warm rice pudding.

I took in a deep breath. His skin had a sharp smell, like burning tar.

"Phew," Chris murmured, holding his nose. He dropped down on the edge of my bed and watched as I started to give Bim a back rub.

The skin on his back turned yellow when I pressed it. His back began to sweat, and the bumps all up and down it appeared to move.

"Nice," Bim whispered. He closed his eyes and grinned. "More. Bim like many back rubs. It makes my feeling happy."

It makes MY feeling sick! I thought.

But I knew it was better to keep him feeling

happy than feeling sad. I turned and glanced at the wood shavings on my rug. I really wanted to cry. I love my dolls. How could he *do* that?

I rubbed Bim's back and shoulders until my hands hurt. The tarry smell was on my hands and on my clothes. I wondered if it would ever come off.

Chris wasn't helpful at all. He just sat there on my bed, watching. I hoped he was thinking of a plan to get this creepy alien out of our house.

Bim had already ruined Kelly's party. Now he was planning to ruin our lives.

Finally, Bim opened his mouth, and a *whoosh* of air escaped his throat.

I jumped back. I thought he was puking up that dead bird again. But no. "Bim yawn," he said. "Back rub make Bim sleepy."

He yawned again, a long explosion of air.

He climbed to his feet and turned to me. "You take good care Bim," he said. "Bim like many back rubs."

"Uh . . . yeah. Sure," I replied.

I felt sick. My hands were damp and achy. And they stunk of tar.

"My feeling is sleepy," Bim said, stretching his arms above his head.

He crossed the room to my bookcase. He squatted down and began pulling all the books from the bottom shelf. He tugged them out three or four at a time and heaved them into the center of the room.

Then he climbed into the shelf and stretched out on his back. He yawned again, then settled himself on the wooden shelf.

A few seconds later, his eyes were closed. He was breathing noisily, grunting in a steady rhythm, sound asleep.

Chris stepped around the pile of books. He tiptoed over to me. "Give Chris back rub!" he whispered. Then he broke up, giggling.

"Shut up," I said. I rubbed my tar-smelling hands over his cheeks.

He jumped back and nearly fell over the scattered books. "Oh, wow. That *reeks*!"

"No jokes," I whispered. "We've got to think."

"Come to my room, Meg." He pulled me to the hall. "We can't tell Penny. But we can call Mom and Dad."

"But what makes you think they'll believe us?" I asked. I followed him into his bedroom.

As always, it was a total disaster area. Piles of balled-up dirty clothes on the floor, an empty pizza box, soda cans, game cartridges, and DVDs strewn everywhere.

Chris isn't exactly a neat freak.

"We're going to tell Mom and Dad that an alien named Bim from the Weirdo planet landed in our neighborhood just in time for Halloween?" I said. "He's a little orange guy with three fingers on each hand. And he's in our house and won't leave?"

"Why wouldn't they believe that?" Chris replied. He laughed.

But his smile faded quickly. He dropped onto the edge of his bed and cupped his head in his hands. "They'll never believe any of it," he murmured. "We'll never get rid of him."

16

We tried calling our parents anyway. They didn't answer.

I let out a long sigh. "I'm so tired. What time is it?"

Chris squinted at his phone. "It's after one in the morning." He yawned. "Guess I'm tired, too. Too tired to think straight."

"We'll think of a good plan in the morning," I said. "Our brains will be sharp."

Chris frowned. "I hope."

I thought about going back to my bedroom with a dangerous space alien snoring away. A space alien who eats *living flesh*!

My chest felt fluttery. My heart was hammering. I almost started to cry. "I . . . I don't want to go back there," I said in a trembling voice.

"Bim is sound asleep," Chris said. "He won't bother you. Besides, he likes you — remember? The back rub?"

"Ugh. Don't remind me," I groaned.

He pushed me gently toward the door. A few seconds later, I heard his bedroom door close behind me. Then I heard a click as he locked it.

Since when did he lock his door?

Since Bim moved in, I guessed.

I crept back into my room. Bim was stretched out on his back on the bottom shelf of the bookcase. He had his hands crossed on top of his stomach. He was grunting and snoring and making disgusting, wet throat noises as he slept.

I changed my sheets and grabbed an extra blanket from the closet. Then I turned off the lights and climbed into bed.

I shut my eyes and tried not to think about Bim. But it was impossible. He was just a few feet away from me. And he was so *noisy*!

I pushed my fingers into my ears to try to keep out the snores and grunts. But *no way* could I sleep with my fingers in my ears.

I thought about Kelly. What did she tell her parents when they got home and saw the house totally wrecked? What did her parents say to *her*?

What a frightening, horrible night.

I turned onto my side and tried counting backward from one hundred to one, slowly. Finally, I must have drifted off to sleep.

When I opened my eyes, bright yellow sunlight

poured through the bedroom window. I blinked. Sat up. Tried to shake my head awake.

It took a few seconds for my brain to get started. But then I remembered Bim.

I gazed down at the bottom of the bookcase.

Empty.

"Huh?" I sat straight up and pushed down the covers.

I gazed all around the room. "Bim?"

No sign of him.

The books were still scattered in the middle of the floor. The room still smelled like tar.

"Bim? Are you here?"

I jumped up and looked in the closet. I searched all around the room. I even looked under my desk.

Bim was gone.

Gone for good?

My heart was pounding hard. I did a happy little dance, leaping into the air.

Yes! Yes! Maybe he *was* gone for good. Gone from my house. Maybe he decided he didn't like it here and hurried back to his planet.

I hummed happily to myself as I pulled on a white top and a pair of khaki pants. I couldn't wait to tell Chris the good news.

I brushed my hair quickly. Some of the vampire mascara was smeared on my face. I decided I'd wash it off later.

"Chris!" I shouted as I ran out of my room. "Chris! Hey — Chris! Bim is gone!"

Chris wasn't in his room. I tore down the stairs.

"Chris? Hey!"

I took a few steps into the living room and stopped. And stared in horror.

"Oh, noooo," I moaned. "Oh, no!"

Penny's precious goldfish bowl.

It was *empty*.

17

"Bim," I muttered. "Bim eats only living meat."

Does that include fish?

I couldn't take my eyes off the empty fishbowl. My legs started to tremble, and my knees felt weak.

"Oh, wow," I muttered. "Oh, wow. This is so *horrible*."

I heard shuffling footsteps and turned from the empty fishbowl. Penny walked in from the kitchen. She had a dish towel in one hand and a spatula in the other.

"Meg?" She squinted at me. "I didn't hear you come down. What a beautiful Saturday morning!"

She sounded so cheerful and happy. I took a deep breath. I had to tell her the sad news.

"Uh . . . Penny. Your fish —" I pointed to the empty bowl.

Her mouth dropped open. She seemed so

delicate. I hoped the shock wouldn't be too much for her.

I started across the room to her, in case she fainted or something. "Your fish . . . uh . . . they're not in the bowl . . ." I stammered. "You see —"

"Yes, I know," Penny said calmly. "I moved them to another bowl so I can clean this bowl later."

"You — you — *what?*" I stammered.

"Yes, I clean the bowl twice a day," Penny said. "They complain if the water gets dirty."

"They do?" I murmured, still shaking.

Penny nodded. She waved the spatula toward the kitchen door. "The fish are in the kitchen. Arlo is in a very peppy mood. He's swimming laps in the new bowl. He's a very good swimmer."

Most fish are! I thought. I started to feel a little better.

She waved the spatula again. "Now, why am I carrying this thing?" She knotted up her face. "Hmmmmm. I know I'm carrying it for a reason."

"Are you cooking something for breakfast?" I asked, trying to be helpful.

"Yes! That's it!" Penny cried. "Come have your breakfast, Meg. I'm making blueberry pancakes."

"They smell great, Penny," I said, following

her. My heart was still pounding. I couldn't stop thinking about Bim.

I gazed all around the room as I walked. I expected him to pop up from behind a chair or out of a closet.

I stopped at the kitchen door and quickly glanced around. Was he sitting at the counter?

No.

Meg, calm down! I scolded myself.

Maybe he's gone. Really gone.

Chris sat at the counter. "Where is he?" he whispered.

"Gone," I whispered back.

Chris pumped a fist in the air and gave a cheer.

"You're in a good mood this morning," Penny said to Chris. She dipped the spatula into the frying pan and flipped a pancake high into the air.

It landed on top of her head with a soft *plop*.

"Where did it go?" she asked, squinting all around. "Where did that one get to?"

"I think I'll just have cereal this morning," Chris said.

After breakfast, Chris followed me up to my room. "Wow. Your room is a total mess," he said. "Why don't you keep your books in the bookcase?"

73

"Very funny," I said. "Just cross your fingers that Bim doesn't come back."

Chris held up both hands. "See? I've already got them crossed."

"I'm going to put all the books back," I said. "Then I'm going over to Kelly's and see how she's doing this morning."

Chris walked over to my desk. He reached over and picked up the Floig, the silly little figure I got at HorrorLand. He squeezed its belly and made its eyes pop out.

That made him laugh. Then he bent its spindly legs so the Floig looked like it was sitting on the arm of my chair.

"This little dude is awesome," Chris said. "It feels so good to squeeze him. Wish I'd bought one."

"You heard what that shop owner said," I replied. "He said this was the only Floig he'd ever seen."

Chris squeezed the thing again. "Look. If you push his back, his tongue sticks out." Chris made the Floig's tongue poke out two or three times. He thought it was a riot.

"Meg, can I have him?" he asked.

"No way," I said. I grabbed it out of his hands. "He's part of my doll collection now."

Chris made a disgusted face. "How about we share him?"

I rolled my eyes. "Are you crazy? How can you

even *think* about toys when we have a dangerous alien from outer space in the house?"

Chris glanced around the room. "You said he was gone. Maybe he went back to his planet."

"Or maybe he just went to throw a few stink bombs in people's houses," I said. "You heard what he said. That he's staying with us forever and ever."

Chris sighed. "Maybe we should call 911. Call the police. Or the fire department."

I shook my head sadly. "They wouldn't believe us, either. They'd think it was some kind of Halloween prank."

"Yeah. For sure," Chris muttered. "I'm glad the alien is in *your* room. He totally stinks!" He stood up, crossed the room, and disappeared down the hall.

I searched around for a hiding place for the Floig. I didn't want Chris to steal it. Finally, I tucked it under the sweaters in my bottom dresser drawer.

Then I found Penny, still in the kitchen. She was feeding her three fish with a tiny spoon.

"What are you feeding them?" I asked.

"Goldfish crackers," Penny said. "You know. Those little crackers shaped like goldfish. They love them."

She squinted into the bowl through her thick glasses. "But Arlo isn't hungry this morning," she said softly. "Hope he isn't coming down with a cold."

"Hope not," I muttered. "I'm going to Kelly's house. Back before lunch."

I walked to Kelly's house. It was a gray morning. The air felt cold and wet. The grass was still glistening with frost.

Someone had dropped a red Halloween mask in the grass. A big brown bug was exploring it.

I climbed Kelly's front stoop. A sheet of plastic covered the broken front window.

I raised my hand to ring the bell — and stopped. Kelly's front door was open.

I could hear Bubba barking ferociously inside the house.

My heart skipped a beat.

What was his problem?

Did something else happen?

I took a deep breath. Then I pulled the door open wider.

My legs shook as I took a step into the front room.

And heard Kelly screaming — shrieking in horror, again and again.

"Kelly? What *is* it? What's *wrong*?" I called.

18

The dog was barking so loudly, I didn't know if Kelly could hear me.

I tore up the stairs two at a time. My shoes thudded on the wooden steps. I burst into Kelly's room. "Kelly — what *is* it?"

Kelly had her hands pressed to her face. Her eyes were wild. She was staring down at her bed.

I followed her gaze — and saw why she was screaming. A dead rabbit! Its skin chewed and ripped, red meat poking out wetly. The rabbit corpse lay stretched out on her pillow.

I stumbled across the room. I couldn't take my eyes off the hideous dead thing. One ear had been chewed off. The other ear hung by a thread. The eyes were missing. The entire rabbit was covered in a slimy mucus.

"W-why?" Kelly stammered. "Why? Why?"

I wrapped her in a hug. Her whole body was trembling.

She pulled angrily away from me. She balled her hands into tight fists. "Why is someone doing this to me?" she said, sobbing. "I don't understand what's going on."

The dead rabbit smelled putrid. I tried to pull Kelly away. But she wouldn't budge.

"First the stink bomb ruins my party," Kelly said, shaking her head. "Then I find this disgusting, slimy dead rabbit on my bed. Who is doing these things to me?"

Of course, I had a pretty good idea who the culprit was. It had to be Bim.

But — why?

I helped Kelly dump the ripped-up rabbit corpse into a trash bag. We carried it out to the metal trash cans behind her garage.

"I . . . I have to throw out my pillow, too," she stammered. "And my bedspread." She shuddered. "Every time I go to bed, I'll think of that ugly thing."

"We'll find out who did it," I said. "And we'll stop them." I promised to call her later. Then I hurried out of her house.

So that proved it. Bim wasn't gone. I had to find him. I had to tell him to stop doing these horrible things to my friend.

I felt so totally angry. I wanted to scream at him and tell him he *had* to leave and never come back.

I was so worked up, I bumped right into someone on the sidewalk. Carlos!

"Hey!" We both uttered startled cries.

He wore a black-and-gold *Star Trek* sweatshirt and faded jeans torn at the knees. He had a black wool ski cap pulled down over his ears. He carried a stack of Netflix envelopes in one hand.

"Meg, what's your problem?" he said.

"I'm glad it's you," I said. "I mean, you're the only one who would understand."

He squinted at me. "What are you talking about?"

His house was across the street. I pulled him onto his front stoop and we sat down side by side on the top step.

The cold breeze made me shiver. But I didn't care. Carlos was totally into sci-fi and fantasy. He was the only one I could tell about Bim.

"Carlos, I'm not making this up," I said. "On the way to Kelly's party last night, Chris and I ran into this . . . this alien from another planet."

Carlos laughed. "Meg, it's not April Fool's. It's Halloween," he said.

I stared hard at him. "Do I look like I'm joking?" I said. "Just shut up and listen."

I told him about pulling the little orange dude from the hedge. How he said his name was Bim, and he was a Weirdo. I told Carlos about the stink bomb . . . about finding Bim in my room. . . .

I told Carlos everything. He listened silently. He had a grin frozen on his face.

"Nice try, Meg," he said when I finished. "But *no way* I'm going to believe any of that."

"Carlos, I'm begging you to believe me," I said. "Listen. Could I make this up? Bim goes totally by his feelings. When he's feeling happy, he does happy things. But if he is feeling *unhappy*, his whole personality changes."

"What does he do?" Carlos asked, still grinning.

"He turns evil," I said. "He chewed one of my best antique dolls into sawdust. And I just came from Kelly's house. Bim left a putrid, chewed-up dead rabbit on her pillow."

Carlos burst out laughing. "That's good, Meg. Very good."

I punched him in the knee. "You don't believe me — do you?"

"Of course not," Carlos said. He waved the envelopes in front of me. "I have to go mail these. Have you seen *Stomach Churner III*? It's awesome."

I jumped to my feet. "I'm telling you the truth!" I shouted. "I need your help, Carlos. I really do have a disgusting alien living in my house!"

I grabbed his hands and tugged him to his feet. "Come on. I'll prove it to you."

I dragged him to my house. I pulled him up the stairs. If Bim had returned home, I knew he'd be in my room.

I stopped outside the doorway. Carlos walked into the room ahead of me.

A second later, I heard Carlos let out a loud gasp. And then I heard his cry of horror. "Nooooo! I don't believe it! Nooooo!"

19

I dove into the room.

I saw Carlos standing with both hands pressed over his mouth. And I saw Bim. He was sitting cross-legged on my bed.

And what was he eating? Gobbling so noisily?

A dead squirrel.

I swallowed hard. I shook my head as if trying to shake the picture of him away.

I saw gray fur and pink-and-yellow squirrel guts all over my carpet.

Carlos made a gagging sound. Beneath the ski cap, his eyes were bulging. He let out a moan.

"I . . . don't . . . believe this," he choked out.

On the bed, Bim opened his mouth in a sickening wet burp. He spit a slender squirrel bone against the wall.

"I feel . . . sick," Carlos murmured. He really did look green.

I watched Bim shove the whole squirrel down his throat head first. The back legs disappeared into his mouth. He jammed the tail down his throat. Then he burped again.

"Carlos, *now* do you believe me?" I asked.

He shut his eyes. "Meg, there's something you don't know about me," he whispered.

"What's that?"

"I'm a total coward."

He spun away. And still covering his mouth with both hands, he lurched out of my bedroom. I heard him running down the stairs.

Bim licked his orange lips. He smiled at me. "My feeling is happy," he said.

I heard a noise at the door. I turned to see Chris walk in. "Hey, what's Carlos's problem?" he asked. "He went running past me —"

Chris stopped when he saw Bim.

Bim smiled at him. He held up a piece of squirrel bone. "Want a lick?"

"Oh, nooo," Chris groaned. "Look at this mess."

"It's squirrel," I said.

"Living meat," Bim chimed in. "Nothing taste as good."

Bim slid off my bed. He rushed toward me carrying a meaty squirrel rib. "Taste," he said, shoving it in my face.

"*Aaack!* No!" I cried. I tried to back away.

"Taste!" Bim cried. "Taste!"

He jammed the disgusting bone into my mouth. I could feel the soft, wet squirrel meat against my tongue.

"AAAAACK!" Gagging, I squirmed away.

"Taste good," Bim said, taking the bone back and licking it. "Bim only heave it up twice."

My stomach lurched. I could still taste the putrid squirrel meat. I knew I'd never forget the sick, sour taste.

"You try again," Bim said, waving the rib bone in front of me. "You like."

"Bim, please —" I murmured. I closed my mouth tightly and swallowed again and again, trying to keep my breakfast down.

Bim strode back to the bed and began stuffing the squirrel bone into his mouth.

I turned to Chris.

"Are you okay?" he asked.

"No," I said. "But we have to clean this mess up before Penny sees it."

"I'll get the broom and a dustpan," Chris said.

Bim ripped the last piece of squirrel meat from the bone. Then he let out another loud wet burp. He slid down from my bed. "I brought happy gift," he said to me.

I squinted at him. "A *what?*"

"Happy gift," Bim said. "To your friend, Kelly the girl." He smiled. "Your friend mine friend now. So I brought happy gift."

I let out an angry scream. "The dead rabbit! You thought that was a *happy* gift?"

He nodded. The little antennae on his head wriggled as he grinned.

"You — you're a *menace*!" I shrieked. "That wasn't a happy gift! That was *horrible*!"

His eyes bulged.

"You'll make me lose all my friends!" I screamed.

I totally lost it. I threw myself at Bim and began pounding his chest with both fists. "Go away! Go AWAY!" I shouted. "Please — go away! We don't want you here! Do you understand? We don't *want* you here!"

I tried to pound him some more. But to my horror, both of my fists stuck to his sticky, damp skin.

I struggled to pull them off. But they stuck tight. "Let go of me!" I wailed. "Let go of my hands!"

Bim shook his head. His antennae drooped over his orange forehead. "My feeling very unhappy," he said in a mopey little voice.

"Let go! Let go!" I demanded. I pulled back with all my strength.

POP!

My hands came free. I staggered back. I stared at my hands — and gasped.

They were covered with big ugly warts.

20

"My feeling VERY unhappy!" Bim exclaimed. He grabbed the lamp off my desk and smashed the lightbulb in one hand. Then he tossed the shattered glass across the room.

Chris came back to my room carrying a broom.

"He's ... he's a MONSTER!" I screamed to him. "Look at me! Look at my hands! They're covered in big red warts!"

I grabbed Chris's shoulders and pushed him out into the hall. I followed him and slammed the bedroom door behind me.

I tugged Chris into his room and shut the door. "What are we going to do?"

He swallowed hard. He suddenly looked very afraid.

"Tonight is Halloween," I said. "We're supposed to go trick-or-treating with Kelly and Carlos. We're supposed to have fun. But ... but ..." I started to sputter.

I took a deep breath and held it. But it didn't calm me down.

"We're supposed to have fun tonight," I started again. "But how can we with this disgusting creep in our house, destroying everything?"

"You're right," Chris said in a whisper. He shook his head.

"We have to get him out of the house," I continued. "Before he totally ruins our lives."

Chris blinked. His face suddenly brightened. "Meg, I think I have a plan," he said.

I stared at him. "A plan?"

He nodded. "We'll take him with us to a Halloween party."

My mouth dropped open. "Huh? Have you totally lost your mind? How will that help us get rid of Bim?"

"We'll lose him," Chris said. "I know we can."

I still didn't get it. "Lose him at the party?"

"Yeah," Chris said. "See? We get into our costumes. We tell him to come meet our friends at the great party we've been invited to. We tell him it's way across town, right?"

"Right," I said. "So?"

"So . . . we take him on the craziest, most confusing trip of his life to get across town. First we take the bus to the town center. We get off and take the Metro back in the other direction. Then we take another bus. We zig and we zag, see. We walk in circles for an hour. We get him totally turned around. Then we dump him at some party. And we run as fast as we can."

I scrunched up my face and thought hard about it. "I'm not sure, Chris. . . ."

"It *has* to work!" Chris said. "Bim said he's never been on this planet before — right? We'll get him totally lost. No way he'll ever find his way back to our house."

I shook my head. "Nice try," I said. "But I think your plan is a loser."

"Huh? A loser?"

"It won't work," I said. "We need to keep thinking." I sighed. "There's *got* to be a good way to get rid of an alien from another planet!"

Chris frowned. "I'll keep thinking. We can do it. I know we can."

I turned and slumped back to my room. *Maybe I'll just beg Bim again*, I thought. *Maybe I'll just beg him to go somewhere else.*

But when I opened the door to my room, he was gone.

The window was open wide. The curtains were fluttering. The bedspread was wrinkled where Bim had been sitting.

"Bim? Are you here?"

No answer.

I started for the window to close it. But my eyes caught the shelves on the wall — and I stopped with a sharp cry.

Empty. The shelves were *empty.*

"Where are my dolls?" I shrieked.

And then I saw the low piles on the carpet. At first, I thought it was sand. I bent down to examine them. Not sand.

Sawdust.

All of my dolls. All! Even Elizabeth!

All fifty of them — chewed into wood shavings.

21

At dinner that night, I tried to act normal. The warts had faded on my hands. But every time I thought about my beautiful doll collection, I had to fight back tears.

That monster Bim destroyed my favorite things. I wanted to grab him by his scrawny neck and shake him.

Even Penny noticed that I wasn't myself. "You're not eating your cauliflower, Meg," she said, her face wrinkled with concern.

"We're not having cauliflower," I reminded her.

She shook her head and laughed. "You're right. I *meant* to make cauliflower. Guess I forgot."

Chris sat across from me, eating silently. I could see he was upset, too. He knew how much I treasured those dolls.

After dinner, I hurried up to my room. First, I made sure Bim wasn't around. Then I sat down on the edge of my bed and punched in Carlos's number on my cell phone.

"I'm downloading a movie," he said. "Have you seen *Scrunchers*? It's supposed to be totally gross and sickening."

"How can you think about horror movies when I have an alien living in my room?" I demanded.

"I . . . I'm trying not to think about that," he replied. "I mean, I almost tossed my dinner. Really. I just keep thinking about that slimy dead squirrel."

"You ran away fast enough," I said angrily. "I thought you were my friend."

"I *am* your friend," Carlos said. "But I don't want to be that *thing's* friend! Or his lunch."

"Huh?" I gasped. "You really think he eats *people*?"

"You think he *doesn't*?" Carlos snapped back. "He's an alien from another world. Meg, you don't know what he eats. Or how dangerous he is."

I groaned. "Carlos, I called you for help. And maybe a little cheering up. I don't need to be even more scared!"

"How can I help?" Carlos asked. "You think I could scare him away in my two-headed-alien costume?"

"No, I don't," I said. "I called you because you're a sci-fi freak — right?"

"You mean I'm a geek?"

"I didn't say that. You're an expert. You know stuff. You watch more sci-fi and horror films than any living human. You're downloading *Scrunchers*, right? It's supposed to be the pits!"

"You think? Worse than *Munchers*? Did you see *Munchers*?"

"Give me a break, Carlos," I snapped. "I called you because maybe you have an idea for me. You know. How to get rid of an alien. You must have read a book or watched a movie about getting rid of aliens."

"Usually, you blast them with laser rays," Carlos said.

I groaned again. "Have you got any laser rays handy? *Uggggh*. I'm going to hang up. Are you going to help me or not?"

"Let me think . . ." Carlos replied. "I've read some books with this plot."

"It's not a plot," I said. "It's my life."

I raised my eyes to the empty shelves and the little piles of sawdust on my rug, and I almost cried again.

"Uh . . . well . . ." Carlos was thinking hard, trying to remember. "Maybe if you don't believe in him, he'll go away."

"That's lame," I said. "You're thinking about Tinkerbell or something. It's too late for that. I already believe in him. He's in my room. Ruining my life."

Carlos was silent for a long moment. "Well . . . Meg, you said he's totally controlled by his feelings, right?"

"Right," I said. "He's always talking about how he's happy or how he's unhappy. Always talking about his feelings."

"So? What if you totally *hurt* his feelings?" Carlos said. "You know. Really put him down. Tell him what an ugly little creep he is. Maybe if you really hurt him, he'll get the hint and scram."

I didn't have to think about that. "No way," I said. "If I hurt his feelings, he'll chew me up the way he chewed up my dolls. He's dangerous, Carlos. Too dangerous to play that kind of mind game. He . . . he crushed a lightbulb in his hand!"

"I get it. He's a bad dude," Carlos said.

"I don't think you're taking this seriously," I said.

"Yes, I am," Carlos replied. "We'll think of something, Meg. But what are you going to do in the meantime?"

I sighed again. "Guess I'm going to be nice to him. You know. Keep him feeling happy. So he doesn't wreck my whole house. Or hurt me."

I heard a scrambling at the open bedroom window. I looked up and saw Bim leap into my room.

He had brown stains down his chin and down the front of his blue shirt. His tiny raisin eyes glowed as he grinned at me.

I clicked the phone shut. "You're back," I murmured.

93

"Yes. Keep Bim happy," he said. "Good idea. Keep Bim feeling happy. Very nice."

"You were listening to what I said on the phone?" I asked.

"Know how keep Bim feelings happy?" he asked, walking over to me. He was so light, he made no sound when he walked.

"Keep Bim feelings happy, Megs. Rub Bim's back again."

I blinked. "Excuse me?"

He started to pull his blue shirt over his head. His orange chest was smooth and hairless and damp with big sweat droplets.

"Rub Bim's back again, Megs. Scratch and rub Bim's back hours and hours. Every day." He uttered an ugly giggle. It sounded like choking.

He tossed his shirt onto the bed and turned his back to me.

His skin still smelled like hot tar. I held my breath.

I raised my hands. The warts had faded away. If I touched his skin again, would they come back? Would my whole body be blistered with ugly warts?

"Rub Bim's back. Rub Bim's back." He started to chant, squatting up and down.

I didn't have a choice. I lowered my hands to his shoulders.

Oh, yuck.

Bim rolled his shoulders and kept squatting up and down as I rubbed his lumpy skin. "My feeling is happy," he said.

Then he started to coo like a pigeon. "Coo cooooooo."

I shut my eyes and rubbed up and down his back.

"My feeling is happy," he repeated. "I feeling so happy, I invite my friends. More Weirdos."

"Excuse me?" I cried. I dropped my hands and took a step back. "What did you just say?"

Bim turned and flashed a toothy grin at me. "I invite my friends here. More and more. They come. They live here. All together. In this house. And all will belong to you, Megs. You and the brother. Forever!"

I took another step back. "Noooo," I moaned.

"Yes," Bim said, still grinning. "And you will give many, many back rubs. To all Bim's friends. Many back scratches and rubs all day. And all will be feeling happy."

My mouth hung open. I couldn't hide my horror. The room started to spin. I had to get out of there.

I turned and ran without saying a word. I ran down the hall and burst into my brother's room. Chris was on the edge of his bed, hunched over his cell phone, texting someone, I guessed.

"Okay. Let's try it!" I said breathlessly.

He punched a few more keys, then looked up. "Try it? Try what?"

"Let's try your idea," I said, still panting. "Take Bim to a party across town. And lose him there."

Chris squinted at me. "You really want to try it?"

"We have to do *something*!" I cried.

22

We said good night to Penny and stepped out of the house. A strong wind made the trees bend and whisper. Dead leaves clattered down the sidewalk. A long, sad animal howl from somewhere nearby sent a cold shudder to the back of my neck.

I was back in my vampire costume. My cape fluttered behind me in the wind. I had a silvery mask over my eyes. I kept tasting the thick black lipstick on my mouth.

Chris couldn't find both of his *Star Trek* ears, so he had to come up with another costume. Tonight, he painted his face green and said he was a frog. He wore a green sweater. And that was his whole costume.

We told Bim he was lucky — he didn't need a costume. Kids would think he was already dressed up. That made him chuckle for some reason.

Chris and I kept him between us as we made

our way to the bus stop. He had to keep his little legs churning fast to keep up with us. He kept glancing all around, and his antennae stood straight up.

"Bim, are you excited?" I asked. "You're going to your first Halloween party."

"There will be living meat?" Bim replied.

"Oh, wow. You're hungry?" Chris said.

Bim nodded. "Living meat. Bim needs living meat at a party."

"Sure. No problem," I said. "You can have all the living meat you can eat."

He laughed. "Bim's feeling is happy."

Chris and I kept to the plan. We took the city bus downtown. Then we transferred to another bus and rode it back to our neighborhood.

No one on the buses paid any attention to Bim. One of the drivers told him what an awesome costume he was wearing.

"Bim going have living meat," Bim told the driver.

The driver just laughed.

We climbed off the second bus and walked for blocks in one direction. It was a neighborhood of dark old houses. The wind blew over a garbage can. The metal lid clanged on the sidewalk as it bounced past us.

We turned and circled back. We passed the same dark houses two or three times. Then we walked into Madison Park and crossed back and forth through its winding paths.

"Living meat. Living meat," Bim said, breathing hard. I think this was a lot of walking for the little creature. "Where is party?"

"It's far away," Chris said. "But we're almost there."

We pulled him into the Metro and took it across town. Then we zigzagged down street after street.

Chris may be right, I thought. *Bim will never find his way back after this. Even I am lost!*

Finally, we stopped outside a house where a big Halloween party was taking place. It was an enormous house hidden by tall hedges. The hedges were decorated with orange pumpkin lights. Creepy music played across the wide front lawn.

Cars jammed the long driveway. Two scarecrows guarded the curving walk to the front door. The door was covered in thick cobwebs.

We heard laughter and loud voices inside. Through the tall front windows, I could see a big crowd of people in costumes.

We walked Bim into the house. No one stopped us.

The roar of voices and music made his antennae shoot straight up. He staggered back a step. "This is party?" he asked.

I nodded. "Yes. This is a party. Lots of people talking and dancing and having fun."

"And they eat living meat?" Bim asked.

"Yes. Lots of living meat," Chris said.

Chris and I led the way through the big front room. The lights were down low. Jack-o'-lanterns along the wall gave only flickering light.

This party was perfect for losing Bim.

After a few minutes, I felt Chris tug my arm. "Quick. Let's run," he said into my ear. "Look."

He pointed. I squinted hard into the dim, dancing light. I saw Bim at the far wall. He was talking to two girls in silvery robot costumes.

"Perfect," I whispered.

We squeezed through the crowd, heading to the front door. I glanced back a few times. Bim didn't see us. He was talking intensely with the space-robot girls.

Chris and I dove out the front door and tore down the front lawn. I stopped at the tall hedges and gazed back one last time. No sign of Bim.

"We did it," Chris whispered. "I knew my plan would work."

"We'll see," I said. My heart was still fluttering in my chest.

What would Bim do when he realized Chris and I had left him there?

Would he follow some other kid home?

Would he realize he wasn't wanted and fly back to his own planet?

We took a bus back to our neighborhood. Chris was laughing and singing to himself. I stayed silent. I had my fingers crossed on both hands, wishing we'd never see the horrible alien again.

We climbed off the bus and walked the six blocks home. Chris was jumping around, doing a crazy dance.

"I'm a genius," he sang. "Admit it, Megs."

"Don't call me Megs!" I snapped.

"Admit it," he repeated. "I'm a genius."

I stopped and uttered a soft cry. I grabbed Chris and pointed.

"Okay, genius," I said. "Who's that standing at our front door?"

Not Bim. A clown and a two-headed alien.

Kelly and Carlos.

Kelly had changed her costume from the night of the party. But I recognized her face behind the white face paint.

They both came running up to Chris and me. Carlos's two heads bobbed crazily as he ran. "Where were you?" he called.

"I thought we had a plan to trick-or-treat," Kelly said.

I let out a sigh. "Oh, wow. I completely forgot we were meeting you. It's a long story," I said.

"Carlos has been telling me one of his crazy sci-fi stories," Kelly said. "About a space alien that lands in our neighborhood."

"It's not a crazy story," I said. "Come inside and we'll tell you what's been going on."

I led them around the back, and we went in the kitchen door. I didn't hear the TV on. I guessed Penny was in her room.

I tore off my cape and dropped it onto a kitchen chair.

"Come up to my room," I said. "I don't want to disturb Penny."

"Got any Halloween candy?" Carlos asked. "I could use a Snickers bar."

"How can you think about candy when my whole life could be ruined?" I said.

"I always think about candy," Carlos replied.

He tugged off his two heads and tucked them under his arm. I led the way up the stairs to my room.

"Whoa. Hold on," Carlos said. "I'm not going up there if that disgusting little alien is still there."

"Alien?" Kelly asked, squinting at me. "You mean he's *real*?"

"We got rid of him," Chris said. "It wasn't easy, but we did it. That's why we weren't home when you arrived."

"You got rid of him? How?" Carlos asked.

I pulled open the door to my room — and screamed.

Bim stood next to my computer, an angry scowl on his orange face.

23

I felt my heart skip a beat. "How did you get here?" I shouted.

Chris, Kelly, and Carlos crowded into the doorway.

"Bim has Weirdo Tracking," he said. His raisin eyes glowed a dark blue. His antennae were spinning wildly on top of his head. "All Weirdos got Weirdo Tracking. Here." He pointed to his belly.

I took a few steps into the room. Chris and our friends hung back in the doorway.

Bim patted his belly. "Bim never get lost with Weirdo Tracking. Go anywhere in universe."

I glanced at Chris. He was shaking his head. I'd *told* him his party plan was lame. Now I knew we were in major trouble.

"My feeling unhappy!" Bim growled. "My feeling ANGRY!"

He scrunched his face tight and started to change. He made sick grunting sounds as his body inflated like a balloon. As I froze in horror, he grew to *twice* his size.

Once again, his orange skin darkened to red. His tiny eyes bulged to the size of Ping-Pong balls. And pointed yellow fangs, covered in drool, slid down from his gums.

"Oh, no!" I heard Kelly cry from the doorway. "This is getting *too scary*!"

Bim opened his mouth in a windy roar. "Why you lose your friend Bim?" he demanded.

Gobs of thick, yellow slime dripped from his fangs onto my carpet. His antennae stood straight and stiff.

"Why leave Bim at party?" he roared. "It makes my feeling sad. Sad and angry."

"Well . . . uh . . ." I stammered.

What could I say? I couldn't think of a reply.

Bim lowered his big round head — and smashed it through my computer monitor.

The shattering glass sounded like a car crash. Glass flew over my desk and rained onto the carpet.

Kelly screamed.

"I'm outta here!" Carlos cried. But he didn't move. He just stood there staring at the angry space alien.

Drool ran down Bim's chin. His chest heaved up and down. He had glittering shards of glass stuck in his forehead.

"My feeling is *angry*," he grunted. A frightening, ugly voice. "My feeling is *so ANGRY!*"

"Bim — please!" I cried.

He dove across the room to my bedroom window. Lowered his head like a battering ram — and butted it through the glass!

Another deafening crash.

Bim staggered back.

I pressed my hands to my mouth and gaped at the jagged hole in the windowpane.

My legs suddenly felt wobbly and weak. A wave of dizziness rolled over me. I sank onto the side of the bed.

This isn't happening!

CRASH!

"Stop it! Stop it! Stop it now!" Chris was screaming.

Bim smashed his head into the wall. The wallpaper tore away. He made a huge hole in the plaster.

"Bim, please —" I moaned. "Please . . ."

His face was a violent red. His glowing eyes bulged and spun. His chest rose up under the blue T-shirt. He was breathing hard, making loud wheezing sounds with each breath.

I screamed as he spun his arms like a windmill. He leaped at my dresser — and smashed his head through the mirror.

"Oh, stop him!" I screamed, tearing at my

hair. "Somebody — stop him! Before he destroys *everything*!"

But no one moved.

We were all too terrified.

And then I let out a cry as I saw Penny shuffle into the doorway. She squinted around the room through her thick glasses.

And then she demanded, "What's all the racket, kids?"

24

Penny's mouth dropped open as the room came into focus. I could see the confusion on her face. She gripped the front of her long housedress.

Chris, Kelly, and Carlos stepped aside as Penny moved into the room.

She blinked several times. Then she pointed to my dresser mirror. "Is that mirror broken?"

Bim paid no attention to her. He let out a roar and charged across the room. He butted his head through the other bedroom window.

The window shattered with a clatter of glass. Shards flew everywhere. I could hear big pieces sliding down the side of the house and crashing to the ground.

Penny raised her fists in the air. "Stop it! Stop it, you fool!" she screamed in a hoarse, high voice. "Stop it — you crazy fool!"

I held my breath as Bim stopped. He turned around. He studied Penny, his eyes moving up and down.

"You stupid idiot!" Penny shrieked, waving her fists. "Look what you've done to this room! Are you crazy? You total idiot!"

Bim took a step back. His antennae wilted on top of his head. He appeared to deflate. His shoulders hunched.

"Look. It's making him small again," Carlos said. "Keep it up. It's working."

"He goes by his feelings," I said. "So maybe insults make him feel small and helpless."

"Bim — you're stupid and ugly!" Chris shouted.

Bim opened his mouth in a soft cry. His head lowered.

"You're a total jerk!" I screamed. "A geek-faced jerk!"

"And you smell bad!" Kelly joined in.

Bim shrunk some more, like a balloon losing its air.

"Your skin feels disgusting and gross!" I shouted. "You stink and you grunt like a pig!"

Bim appeared to fold in on himself, like an accordion closing. He shrunk some more. His whole body started to quiver.

"My feelings are *small*," he said in a tiny, baby-ish voice. "You make Bim feel small."

He clasped his hands in front of him. He kept his head lowered as he shrunk back to his normal size.

"Keep it up!" Kelly said. "Keep it up!"

"You're the ugliest beast I've ever seen!" Carlos shouted.

"And your breath stinks!" Chris added.

"You're stupid and you smell like puke, and everybody *hates* you!" Kelly chimed in.

"You're just a dumb-dumb dummy!" Chris shouted.

Bim let out a weak cry. Then he rolled himself up into a tiny ball on the carpet.

My heart was thudding in my chest. But I was starting to feel a little less frightened. We were winning — and Bim was losing.

I stared at the little orange ball so still on the floor. "Good-bye, Bim," I said. "And good riddance!"

"Good-bye, Bim," Chris, Carlos, and Kelly echoed.

"My feelings are small." Bim's voice came out tiny and weak from somewhere inside his balled-up body.

"My feelings are sad and small," he squeaked. "And when Bim's feelings are small, you know what happens?"

All four of us stared down at him without saying a word.

Was he going to disappear? Vanish into thin air?

"When Bim's feelings small, it makes Bim not

happy," he squeaked. But then his voice suddenly grew deeper, stronger. "It makes Bim's feeling VERY NOT HAPPY!" he roared. **"VERY NOT HAPPY!"**

"Oh, no!" I wailed. "Look *out*!"

25

I stumbled back and nearly knocked Penny over. I saw Kelly and Carlos back up to the wall.

The little orange ball unfolded quickly. Bim stood up ... stood tall ... grew ... spread out FAST. His shoulders popped wide. His chest swelled.

In seconds, he roared back to his big size. He turned angry red again. His eyes bulged like glowing hot rocks. His fangs slid down.

He opened his mouth in a deafening animal roar.

He grew bigger ... bigger. Until his head nearly hit the ceiling.

He was a *monster* now!

I grabbed Penny. Her eyes were wide with terror. Her slender body was shaking. I heard her teeth chatter.

I pulled her down the hall to Chris's room. I thought she'd be safe there. "I'll take care of it,"

I told her. "Don't worry. Try to calm down. I'll take care of it."

Take care of it. What a joke!

"Lock the door," I told Penny. "Lock the door, and you'll be safe."

She was shaking too hard to argue with me.

I closed the door and hurried back into the hall.

"Come on, everyone!" I shouted.

But I didn't have to call them. They were already tearing after me. We bolted down the stairs and out the front door. We didn't stop till we were at the sidewalk.

I struggled to catch my breath. Up in my bedroom, I could hear Bim roaring like an angry lion through the broken windows.

I turned frantically to Carlos. "Insulting Bim didn't work out too well," I said. "Any other ideas?"

Carlos nodded. "Yes. *Run!* He's coming after us!"

Bim burst out of the house, roaring, flailing his gigantic arms, gnashing his dripping fangs. I gaped in horror. He had become a giant *monster*!

He had to be at least ten feet tall. His open-jawed roar made the windows on the front of the house shake.

He grabbed the tree next to the stoop and

ripped it out of the ground. Then he heaved it at us and came running.

"*Bim angry! Bim angry!*" he raged. He stretched his arms out, ready to grab us.

No way could we outrun him. He came at us with big, lumbering strides, frothing and bellowing.

"*Bim angry! Bim angry!*"

He stumbled over a bush and fell heavily over it. With a growl, he picked himself up, turned — and ripped the bush from the ground.

He rolled it out of his way and came running.

"*Bim very ANGRY!*"

"He . . . he's going to catch us," Chris stammered, panting hard.

"What can we do? We can't *fight* him!" Kelly cried.

Bim ripped a mailbox up and flung it across a driveway.

"Back to my house!" I cried. I waved them toward the backyard. "We'll lock ourselves in my room and call 911!"

We started along the side of the house.

"NOOOO!"

I let out a wail of horror as I felt strong arms wrap around my waist.

Bim grabbed me from behind.

I felt his hot breath on the back of my neck. And his sticky drool on the back of my shirt.

He lunged forward and tackled me to the grass.

I tried to scramble out from under him. But he was too heavy, and his grasp was too tight.

"Living meat!" he growled in my ear. "Living meat! My feeling is HUNGRY!"

And then I felt his wet teeth sink into my neck.

26

"Ohhhhhh." A moan escaped my throat.

I clamped my eyes shut and waited for the pain to rush down my body.

But to my surprise, I felt no pain.

I heard Bim growl. Then felt his grip loosen. The weight on top of me lightened.

I took in a deep breath. Opened my eyes. Climbed to my knees.

And gasped in shock. Carlos was holding Bim up in the air. Bim was still huge. But Carlos held him high.

"I don't believe it! He . . . he was so easy to pick up," Carlos said. "Light as a feather!"

Heart pounding, I scrambled to my feet. "Carlos!" I screamed. "Put him down — *fast*! He can make himself weigh a *ton*!"

Too late.

Bim scrunched up his face and let out a loud grunt.

"Whooooaaah!" Carlos cried out in surprise as Bim turned heavy.

And toppled on top of Carlos.

"He . . . he's *crushing* me!" Carlos choked out.

Bim didn't move. The huge alien held his weight on top of Carlos.

Carlos's face turned red, then purple.

"Can't . . . breathe . . ." he groaned. "Help. Can't . . . breathe . . ."

Kelly, Chris, and I moved without saying a word. We dove to Bim's side, lowered ourselves — and pushed. Pushed against Bim with all our strength.

Carlos's eyes were popping. His face was bright blue.

We pushed harder. And somehow we rolled the big monster off our friend. Rolled him like a heavy log.

Carlos groaned. His face slowly returned to its normal color.

Kelly and I grabbed Carlos by the arms and tugged him to his feet. The four of us took off, running full speed toward my house.

I glanced back. Bim was trying to climb up to run after us. But he was so heavy, he couldn't raise his own weight!

He pushed himself off the grass with both hands — then went crashing back to the ground.

I reached the kitchen door first and pushed it open. The four of us scrambled inside.

"My feeling *angry*! My feeling VERY angry!"

I could hear Bim shouting from out front. I slammed the door and locked it.

I was gasping for breath. I think we all were.

But we pulled ourselves up the stairs to my room. Once we were safely inside, I closed the bedroom door and locked it.

Chris and Carlos hurried to my dresser. They each grabbed a side and slid the tall dresser in front of the door.

"That should keep him out," Kelly said. Her whole body shuddered. She hugged herself. "Quick, Meg — call 911."

"Okay," I said. I glanced around the room, searching for my phone.

"Hurry!" Kelly cried. "Please!"

"My . . . my phone," I murmured. I searched the dresser top. Then I checked my desk.

"I . . . don't see it," I said, my voice trembling. "My phone . . ." I turned to the others. "Did anyone else bring a phone?"

They shook their heads.

I crossed the room to my bed and searched the bedspread. "I thought I had it here," I said.

I heard a crash downstairs. We all heard it.

"Meg — he's in the house!" Chris said.

"I can't find my phone," I said, spinning frantically around, my eyes searching everywhere.

Kelly's chin trembled. She hugged herself tighter. "We're trapped in here? We can't call for help?"

I heard thundering footsteps coming up the stairs. I froze. I suddenly felt cold all over.

A deafening *CRAAAASH* rocked the room.

The door burst open. The dresser tilted. Bim shoved it with both hands. It toppled to the floor, drawers spilling out.

Bim stepped over it and gazed at us with an ugly grin.

"Living meat!" he cried.

27

We all stood frozen, gaping at the giant alien as he stomped toward us.

Nowhere to run. Nowhere to hide.

Bim grunted and drooled. His chest heaved up and down. His antennae rocked back and forth on top of his huge head.

I uttered a cry as his fangs slid down. He made loud sucking noises, moving them up and down.

"Feeling hungry, Megs!" he growled.

He took a step toward me. Then another. A gob of thick drool made a *splat* sound as it hit the carpet.

"No — please!" I cried. I saw the terrified faces of Chris and my two friends.

"Leave her alone!" Kelly shouted.

Bim grunted in reply. He took another thudding step forward.

I backed up. My legs were all rubbery and weak. I thought I was going to cave in like a folding chair.

"Living meat!" Bim snarled.

I backed up till I hit my bookcase. I couldn't think. I couldn't move.

Frantic, I grabbed a big hardcover book off the shelf — and heaved it at Bim.

It hit him in the chest and bounced to the floor. He blinked. It seemed to stun him. He shook his head hard.

I grabbed an old history textbook and flung it wildly. It bounced off Bim's leg.

He grunted in surprise. He blinked again. He bent to rub his leg.

I heaved another book. I saw Chris grab a book from my desk. He sent it flying into Bim's side.

Carlos lifted my iPod dock and tossed it at Bim's head.

Bim ducked, but it sailed into his twin antennae.

"My feeling still HUNGRY!" he roared.

I heaved a heavy metal bookend at him. Chris tossed my book bag.

The four of us were throwing everything we could get our hands on.

I don't think it hurt him. But Bim appeared stunned and confused.

I grabbed for another book — and gasped. The shelf was empty. I'd tossed all the books.

Now what?

Chris bounced my computer keyboard off Bim's back.

The big alien growled like a cornered animal — and took another step toward me.

He was only a few feet away. I frantically searched the shelves. Nothing left to throw.

Fat gobs of drool fell from Bim's open mouth. He made that sick sucking sound again with his fangs.

I dropped to my knees in front of a fallen dresser drawer. I desperately searched for something to throw at him. *Anything* to slow him down! *Anything* to keep from being living meat!

I fumbled in the dresser drawer. Under my sweaters, my hand wrapped around the Floig, the funny little doll from HorrorLand. I heaved the thing at Bim's head.

He reached up and caught it in one hand. Then he lowered it slowly in front of his face.

His eyes went wide. He stopped grunting. His fangs slid back up. His mouth hung open.

He stared at the Floig without moving. And suddenly he started to shrink. Bim settled back into his old size — about three feet tall. The orange color returned to his skin. His antennae drooped over his forehead.

When he finally raised his eyes to me, Bim looked like a baby again.

"Now Bim remember!" he said in a soft voice. "Space travel made Bim forget. But now Bim remember why he came here."

He hugged the Floig tightly to his chest.

"Bim been looking everywhere for you!" he told it.

28

I couldn't help myself. A laugh burst from my throat.

I guess it was because I had been so terrified. And because Bim looked so funny cradling that ugly toy in his arms.

All four of us began to laugh. Bim laughed, too, but he had tears in his tiny raisin eyes.

"You came here to find that thing?" I finally asked him.

Bim nodded. "Weirdo Tracking brought me. Because Floig was here. Tracking brought Bim to your house."

"But you forgot what you were looking for?" I asked.

He nodded again. "Space travel mix up Bim's mind."

"But what *is* that thing?" Chris demanded.

Bim rocked it, holding it against his chest like a baby. "Floig I played with when I was tiny Bim. Bim searching and searching for most favorite toy."

Big tears rolled down the alien's cheeks.

"This makes my feeling HOMESICK!" he exclaimed sadly. "Homesick. Very homesick. Bim go home now."

He hugged the Floig tightly to his chest, and he began to spin. Faster . . . He twirled faster and faster like a top picking up speed.

"Good-bye, Megs and the brother," he called. His voice already seemed far away.

Faster. He spun so fast, he became an orange blur.

And then the color faded. Bim vanished with a *whoosh*.

Gone.

I didn't move. I didn't blink. I stared at the spot where he'd spun.

No one said a word.

And then Penny interrupted the silence. She came shuffling into the room. I'd forgotten all about her!

"Did that crazy kid go home?" she asked. "Something is a little *off* about him. His parents should have a long talk with that kid."

We couldn't help it. We burst out laughing.

Penny was very confused. She made her way downstairs to give her fish their midnight snack.

Carlos and Kelly asked if they could help clean up.

I yawned. "Come back tomorrow morning," I said. "I'm too exhausted to start cleaning up tonight."

They went home.

Chris gazed around my destroyed bedroom. "Thank goodness that's over. This was a crazy night," he murmured.

"Crazy night," a tinny, shrill voice repeated.

"Crazy night," another voice echoed.

"Huh?" I uttered a startled gasp. And turned in time to see *three Bims* climb in through the broken window.

Then three more followed them into my room. They were all identical. They looked exactly like Bim!

"Who are you?" I screamed. "What do you want?"

"Bim invite us," one of them said. He grinned at me. "Bim say come."

"Good back rubs," another one chirped. "Bim say good back rubs here."

"Bim invite us," the first one repeated.

"Living meat and good back rubs."

"Bim say to come. Good back rubs every day."

One of them settled down into a dresser drawer on my floor. "We come forever and ever!" he said.

PART THREE

29

What a nightmare! A room full of chattering Bims!

I gaped in horror at the lumpy, smelly, disgusting creatures.

Every time I thought this Halloween couldn't get worse — it DID!

I had to get out of there. I couldn't deal with this. "Chris, let's go!" I cried.

We both started for the bedroom door, but two of the creatures blocked our way.

"Where Bim?" one asked.

"Where Bim? Where Bim?" they all started chanting in their tinny voices.

"Bim isn't here. He left!" I cried. "Bim went home!"

That silenced them. They squinted at me with their tiny raisin eyes.

"Bim go home?"

"Bim home? Don't stay for back rub?"

"Yes. Bim went home," Chris said.

They all began chattering to each other in a strange language that sounded like clicks and burps. Suddenly, they turned silent. They formed a tight circle around Chris and me.

"Chris," I whispered, "I don't like this."

We couldn't duck away. They had us surrounded.

I watched for their fangs to drop down . . . for the Bims to grow huge and angry.

"Sorry," one of them said. His antennae drooped over his forehead. "Sorry. No Bim." He moved closer. His tiny eyes were locked on mine.

I held my breath. What did they plan to do?

"No Bim here," he repeated. "Bim go home. We go home, too."

My mouth dropped open. Huh? *Would they really leave?*

Yes. They began to twirl. Slowly at first, then picking up speed. They spun so fast, the wind almost knocked Chris and me over. The window curtains flew up to the ceiling. The ceiling light rattled and shook.

And then silence. Everything still. They were gone.

My heart pounded. I glanced around my room. It looked like someone had taken one of those big wrecking balls and swung it into everything I owned. What a disaster!

"Bim go home!"

"Oh!" I jumped when I heard a tiny voice behind me.

I spun around. Chris! He laughed. "Bim go home! Bim go home!"

He did a crazy dance around the room. "Bim gone! Bim gone!"

We both cheered and bumped knuckles and danced and celebrated. Then we went down to the kitchen and stuffed ourselves with junk food and Halloween candy.

We had fun — for a little while. But I kept thinking that Mom and Dad would be home in two days. How could I ever explain what happened here?

Finally, we went up to our rooms. I suddenly felt tired, but I knew I'd never get to sleep. I kept glancing at the window, expecting more weird space aliens to come popping in.

My dresser was still lying facedown on the floor. My clothes and books were scattered all over the carpet. My cell phone was on the floor near the door. I picked it up and put it into my pocket. Then I started across the room to see if I could pull a nightshirt from the mess.

And something caught my eye.

A dull yellow-green glow. On the corner of my desk.

I blinked. Was something on fire?

Stumbling over, I lurched to the desk. And stared at the little green-and-purple Horror. The tiny figure the old shop owner had attached to my souvenir package.

As I stared at the glowing figure, I remembered Jonathan Chiller handing me the package. And I remembered his words: *Take a little Horror home with you.*

The Horror glowed with a steady yellow-green light. And as I gazed at it, I suddenly felt strange. Quivery. Dizzy.

I leaned toward the light. I felt myself pulled to it.

And I let out an angry growl. "Stop it! Stop!" I screamed. "Enough! Haven't I had enough scares for one Halloween?"

I felt its warmth. Like standing in front of an open oven. Wave after wave of heat.

"No! Stop! Leave me alone!" I cried.

I grabbed the glowing Horror in both hands. And squeezed it with all my might.

A shock of yellow light shot out around me. Blindingly bright, it wrapped me inside it. Like a bright yellow glove spreading around me, tightening . . . tightening . . .

I let out another cry as I felt myself lifted off the floor.

I tried to toss the glowing Horror away. But it stuck to my hands.

I heard a *whoosh*. A wind blew hard at my back.

The light surrounded me. So bright I had to close my eyes. I clamped them shut tightly and struggled to breathe against the powerful wind that carried me . . . carried me . . . *where*?

Suddenly, the wind stopped. A hush settled around me. I felt the billowing heat fade away.

I opened my eyes slowly. Blinked a few times.

"Where am I?" The words escaped my throat. "Where *am* I?"

30

I expected to see my empty bookcase. My totally wrecked and messed-up room.

But no. I was standing in a brightly lit store. Hunched in a narrow aisle between high, cluttered shelves. I saw grinning skulls . . . a two-headed monkey . . . a fortune-teller's crystal ball . . . giant rubber cockroaches.

"Oh, wow," I muttered. I knew where I was.

I didn't *believe* it. But I knew where I was. Back in Chiller House. Back in HorrorLand.

I heard a cough. I turned to see Jonathan Chiller step out from behind the counter.

His balding head gleamed under the store lights. He peered at me through the square glasses perched on the end of his nose. When a smile slowly crossed his face, his gold tooth glimmered.

"Welcome back, Meg," he croaked in his old-man voice. He took a step toward me.

I took a step back — and bumped into a giant stuffed Godzilla.

"What's going on?" I cried in a trembling voice. "How did I get here?"

His smile grew wider. The shoulders of his old-fashioned brown suit rose up and down. "Magic," he said softly.

He reached for the little Horror. I didn't even realize I still had it gripped tightly in my hand. I handed it to him. He tucked it into his pants pocket.

"I . . . I don't understand," I stammered. "Why did you do this? Why did you bring me back here? Didn't that ugly Floig cause me enough trouble?"

He motioned with one hand. "Take a deep breath, Meg. You are perfectly safe here. I know you've had a surprising time."

"*Surprising?*" I screamed. "You call it *surprising*? It . . . it was *horrible*! I want to go home — now!"

Again, he motioned for me to calm down. "*Shhhh.* You're going to have fun," he said in a whisper. "I brought you here for fun."

I swallowed hard. My mouth was dry as sand. "Fun?"

He swept a hand back over his thinning hair. "Halloween is the most exciting time of all at HorrorLand," he said. "The park is a

135

huge Halloween party. I thought you would enjoy it."

"You grabbed me from my house and pulled me here through some kind of weird magic so I could enjoy Halloween at HorrorLand?" I rolled my eyes. "Tell me another one. What is this *really* about?"

"I'm telling the truth," Chiller said softly. "I love to play games, Meg. I had a lonely childhood. I spent day after day in my room, making up all kinds of games."

I stared hard at him. "Boo hoo," I said. "Will you please send me home now?"

He ignored my question. "I thought you might like to come back here and play a game, too," he said.

I crossed my arms tightly in front of me. "What kind of game?"

His gold tooth gleamed. "A masquerade game," he said. "You know. For Halloween."

"I don't *think* so," I said. "Thanks anyway. I've already celebrated Halloween. How about you send me home now?"

Chiller picked up a stuffed python and pulled it back and forth through his hands. "Don't worry, Meg. I'll send you home safe and sound," he said. "I promise. I'm not a bad man. I just like to share my games with others."

I stared hard at him. "Not interested."

The stuffed python slid through his hands. "It's an easy game," Chiller said. "You just have to do one thing to win."

I rolled my eyes. "One thing? What? What do I have to do?"

His expression grew serious. "Prove that you are you," he said.

31

"Excuse me?"

My mouth dropped open. I leaned back against the counter. "You want to see my I.D.?" I said. "My school I.D.? I don't have it with me. I didn't know I was coming here, remember? I didn't think I'd have to bring I.D.!"

The words tumbled out of me. My heart was thudding so hard in my chest, I could barely hear myself think.

Chiller set the stuffed python down next to a pile of plastic spiders. "No. No need for an I.D. card," he said. "That won't help you, Meg. This is a game."

I took a deep breath and let it out slowly. Outside the shop, I heard kids laughing and shouting to each other.

"The game is called Double or Nothing," Chiller said.

I crossed my arms tighter over my chest. "I told you — I don't want to play."

His eyes narrowed behind the weird square eyeglasses. "You want to go home, don't you?" he said softly.

I felt a chill roll down my back.

He looked so kindly and old-fashioned. Like somebody's grandfather. But was he totally evil? Was he *insane*?

He motioned to the front door. "Go out and have fun, Meg. You'll be amazed at how different HorrorLand is at Halloween time."

"But —" I started.

"Go out there and enjoy it," Chiller said. "And as you explore, you will find a way to win my game. Prove to me that you are *you*, and you will win."

He walked to the front of the shop and squeezed behind the counter.

"Please — tell me what's really going on," I pleaded. "I don't understand your game. What are the rules? If you want me to prove who I am, why are you sending me out into the park?"

"That's part of the game," he said. "You'll see. I expect you to be confused at first. That's the fun of it. But it will all become clear to you."

"But . . . but . . ." I sputtered.

He lowered his head and began going through a tall stack of papers.

I could see he wasn't going to tell me any more. I hurried past him and pushed open the door.

I stepped into Zombie Plaza, crowded and

noisy. Kids and families hurried past, laughing and talking. Everyone seemed to be in a costume.

Glowing orange jack-o'-lanterns hung on all the light poles. None of them had smiles carved on their faces. They all looked angry and menacing.

Creepy music blared from the loudspeakers. Frightening, evil laughter rang out every few seconds.

I didn't want to explore HorrorLand. I knew I had to get out of there.

Penny will go crazy if she wakes up tomorrow morning and I'm not there, I thought.

I knew my parents were on their way home. They'd be frantic when they learned I disappeared.

"No. No way," I said out loud. "I'm outta here!"

With a trembling hand, I pulled my cell phone from my jeans pocket. I raised it to my face. Orange jack-o'-lantern light was reflected on the screen.

I squinted at the keyboard. And punched in my dad's cell number.

It rang once. Twice.

"Come on, Dad. Pick up. Be there. *Please* be there!"

And then I heard: "Hello?"

"Dad — it's me," I said breathlessly. I had to shout over the noise of the crowd. "Dad,

I don't know how to explain this. You'll just have to believe me. But I'm not home. I'm at HorrorLand. I —"

"Meg, don't try to call your parents," a man's voice boomed into my ear.

"Huh?"

I nearly dropped the phone. I squeezed it tighter and pressed it to my ear.

"Wait a minute! You're not my dad! Who *is* this?"

32

"Don't waste time, Meg."

Now I recognized the voice in my ear. Jonathan Chiller.

"Don't waste time trying to escape," he repeated. "Just have fun. Play the game."

"But . . . I don't know what you mean," I said. My voice came out shrill and high. "I don't know how to play. How can I prove to you who I am?"

"You'll find your way," Chiller replied.

"But —"

He clicked off. I stared at the phone for a moment, then tucked it back into my pocket.

My head spinning, I took a few steps into the plaza. The long row of shops was glowing in orange light. A line of people stood outside the mask store.

A gorilla carrying a trick-or-treat bag bumped into me. "Sorry," a boy's voice behind the mask said. And then he added, "Is it really you?"

I stared at him. "Excuse me?"

"Is it really you?" the gorilla repeated. "Have you tried The Haunted Pumpkin?"

"What do you mean?" I demanded. "Tell me what you mean!"

But the gorilla lumbered off, swinging the trick-or-treat bag beside him.

I stopped to let two masked kids on stilts walk by. They were followed by two witches with long, crooked noses.

The park was jammed with kids and families. I saw a two-headed fire-breathing dragon waiting at a water fountain. The two heads reminded me of Carlos and his space alien costume.

I wished Carlos and Chris were here with me now. Maybe they could help me figure out this crazy game of Chiller's so I could get home.

Where should I start? Was that gorilla kid giving me a clue?

A green-and-purple Horror — one of the park guides — held a big sign in front of his furry chest. It had arrows pointing in all directions.

One arrow pointed to THE HALLOWEEN HOUSE OF SCREAMS. Below that, an arrow pointed to THE HALLOWEEN HOPPER. Another arrow pointed to THE HAUNTED PUMPKIN.

The Horror saw me staring at his sign. "Know any good Halloween jokes?" he called to me.

"No," I said.

"Neither do I," he said. He turned and stomped away.

Weird.

I saw a food cart across the way. I suddenly realized I was *starving*. I pushed my way through some ghosts and ugly skeletons and stepped up to the cart.

A Horror in a black apron was turning hot dogs on a grill with a spatula. I gazed down at the sizzling hot dogs. They were black-and-orange!

"Care for a Halloweiner?" the Horror growled. He shoved a bun in my face. "Free for the holiday."

I laughed. HorrorLand really does a big thing at Halloween. Even the food is different.

I bit into the black-and-orange Halloweiner. Not bad at all. Tasted like a regular hot dog. So I had another one and a cup of Apple Spider, which was cider with little candy spiders in it.

The food made me feel a little better. I crossed the plaza and kept walking.

A gigantic jack-o'-lantern — as big as a circus tent — rose up in front of me. Bright yellow light poured out from the jagged eyes and nose and the crooked mouth carved in the front. A blinking sign read: THE HAUNTED PUMPKIN.

The boy in the gorilla costume was giving me a clue, I decided. *I'll go inside.*

I saw a line of kids climbing into the huge

pumpkin through the open mouth. While I waited my turn, a girl in a green lizard costume caught my attention. She stood across the way, next to a light pole, staring at me. She didn't move or glance around. Just stared hard at me through her lizard mask without blinking.

What's up with her? I wondered. I didn't have time to think about it. It was my turn to enter The Haunted Pumpkin. I lowered my head and pushed my way inside.

Hundreds of kids were running around on the soft, gooey floor. They were bouncing off the wet orange walls, laughing, dancing, and goofing around.

The walls were spongy, and pumpkin strings hung down from the top like orange streamers. The pumpkin smell was so real — strong and gross.

My shoes crunched over a thick carpet of white seeds. Pulsing yellow light shone from the pumpkin walls. I could see the sky through the carved-out eyes, nose, and mouth.

In front of me, some kids were furiously tossing handfuls of pumpkin guts at each other. This really felt like being inside a pumpkin!

Suddenly, screams rang out. The giant pumpkin started to tilt. It tilted forward rapidly. Kids stumbled and fell to the soft floor.

The pumpkin rocked from side to side. Then tilted again, forward then back.

It took me a few seconds to realize this was part of the fun. Everyone screamed and laughed. The floor came rolling up — and I stumbled back into a bunch of screaming kids.

The pumpkin rocked again. Kids stumbled and staggered.

I remembered the earthquake my family was in when we visited my aunt in Oakland. I laughed. This was like being inside a pumpkin during an earthquake!

Suddenly, the laughs came to a sharp stop. A hush fell over the pumpkin. Then gasps rang out.

I spun around, dizzy, and saw flames shooting off the back wall. The flames danced high and quickly spread over the back of the pumpkin.

Were these special effects? Part of the pumpkin ride?

The fire crackled. The pale walls were turning black.

Kids stampeded to the jagged mouth. Screams rose over the roaring flames. Running fast over the spongy floor, kids pulled each other to the jack-o'-lantern face. And dove out through the open mouth.

I lowered my head and ran. I could feel the heat of the fire on my back. Someone pushed me hard from behind. I dove to my knees and rolled outside through the pumpkin mouth.

Everyone was screaming and shouting. I climbed to my feet and turned back to the burning pumpkin.

But the flames had stopped. The pulsing yellow light gleamed from the eyes, nose, and mouth openings. The giant pumpkin stood still and silent.

"All a joke!" a boy shouted.

"It's a fake!"

"No fire! No fire!" a girl shouted to her parents. "It's a joke!"

"Awesome! Let's go in again!"

Some kids started back into the jack-o'-lantern. Others hung back, watching them.

I took a deep breath. My heart was still pounding hard. I pulled some pumpkin seeds off the knees of my jeans. I brushed some more off the laces of my sneakers.

When I looked up, a bunch of masked people were watching me.

Was I imagining it?

No. A family of seven, dressed in pirate outfits, were standing perfectly still. They all had their eyes on me.

Two teenage couples wearing *Star Trek* masks walked past. They all turned to gaze at me as they went by. Beside them, I saw the girl in the green lizard costume again. Her tail trailed along the pavement. Her eyes were locked on mine.

I turned and saw a tall Horror, furry arms crossed in front of his overalls, watching me intently.

What's up with this? I wondered.

A shiver ran down my back. *Why is everyone STARING at me?*

33

"Are you wearing a mask?" the Horror asked.

I squinted at him. "What?"

"Are you wearing a mask?" he repeated. And then the family of pirates repeated his question: "Are you wearing a mask?"

As I stared in total confusion, everyone around me began to chant: "Are you wearing a mask? Are you wearing a mask?"

I looked from face to face. *This must definitely be a clue,* I decided. *They must be part of the game.*

Were they telling me to join them? To get a mask?

I could see the mask store across Zombie Plaza. I turned away from the chanting masked faces and started to jog toward the store.

I stepped up to the front of the shop. The sign above the door read: MAKE A FACE!

Blue light glowed in the window. I pressed my nose against the glass and peered in. The display was nearly empty. The masks had almost all been sold.

A shrill scream rang out when I pushed open the front door. I jumped.

A fat Horror behind the counter tossed back his head and laughed a booming laugh. "Did I get you?" he demanded. "Did I get you with that one?"

"Kind of," I said. I blinked in the deep blue light. It was a little like being underwater.

I stepped closer to the counter. I could see that the Horror was wearing a *mask* of a Horror. What a joker.

I gazed around the store. The shelves were nearly empty.

"I need a mask," I said.

The Horror squinted at me through his Horror mask. "What's wrong with the one you're wearing?" His booming laugh rang out again.

"Don't feel bad," he said. "I say that to all the girls."

"Very funny," I said. "I think I need a mask *and* a costume."

He leaned an arm on the counter. "Guess you're the kind of person who likes to plan ahead," he said. "Why wait till the last minute — right?"

This dude was a riot!

"I . . . just got here," I said.

He waved to the costumes hanging on the back wall. "Not much left. See anything you like?"

I walked over to the rack of costumes. In the blue light, I couldn't tell what they were. I pulled a costume off its hanger.

And another shrill scream of horror rang out. I gasped and dropped the costume.

The big Horror laughed. "Just playing with you," he said. "You know. Just doing my job. I used to be an elevator operator. Did I enjoy it? Well, it had its ups and downs!" He roared with laughter.

I pretended to laugh. I mean, I didn't want to hurt the guy's feelings. I just wanted a mask and costume so I could get *out* of there!

I held up the costume. I think it was green. Impossible to tell in the weird light. It had spindly legs and a pinkish tail. "What is this?" I asked.

"You don't want that one," the Horror said. "It's a rat. Besides, that costume is haunted."

My mouth dropped open. "Haunted?"

"Yes, by the ghost of my father."

"I'm so sorry," I said. "Your father died in this costume?"

He shook his head. "No. He's still alive! Ha-ha-ha-ha-ha!"

I let out a frustrated groan. "Do you have anything that will fit me?"

He pulled a bright green costume from under the counter. "This one is for you. It's a lizard." He raised the rubber mask. "Cute, right?"

My mouth dropped open. I recognized it. The same costume that girl in the park was wearing. The girl who stared at me. This was the exact same lizard costume.

"Don't you have anything else?" I asked.

He shook his head.

I sighed and took the costume from him. I slipped it on over my clothes. It had a bumpy back and loose lizard legs that fit over my jeans.

The Horror handed me the mask, and I tugged it down over my head. I adjusted the eye holes so that I could see. And pulled the bottom of the mask down to my lizard neck.

I had to reach under the costume to get to the money in my jeans pocket. I paid the Horror with it.

"Enjoy it, Meg," he said. "You make an awesome lizard."

I started for the front door, then quickly spun around. "Did you just call me Meg?" I demanded. "How do you know my name?"

He stared at me through his Horror mask.

"How do you know my name?" I asked again. "Come on. Tell me. How do you know my name?"

34

He turned away and pretended to be busy with the masks on the counter.

I waited a few more seconds. But I saw that he wasn't going to answer. So I pushed open the door. Heard the shrill scream once again. And wandered onto the plaza.

Is he part of Jonathan Chiller's game? Is that how he knew my name?

I saw a sign pointing to HALLOWEEN TOWN. I started walking toward it and tripped over the bottom of my lizard costume. I hiked the costume up and rolled up the legs so I could walk better.

If only I had some idea of how to play this crazy game. Double or Nothing, Chiller had called it. Well, so far, I had *nothing*. Not a clue.

The path led to a creepy old house. It looked like the haunted house in every scary movie. Its paint was peeling. The windows were all dark. The shutters banged against the walls. A black

153

cat with glowing green eyes peered down at me from the second-floor balcony railing.

A tilted sign on the front porch read: STAY AWAY. HAUNTED. REALLY.

A ghostly howl poured out from a tiny attic window. The floorboards on the porch creaked and groaned as I stepped over them.

This should be fun, I thought. Chris and I love haunted houses. We always talk about turning *our* house into a haunted house for Halloween. But we're always too busy to do it.

A curtain hung over the open front door. I started to step through it before I realized what it was made of. Caterpillars! Fat, furry caterpillars all strung together.

They twisted and squirmed. They were ALIVE! Hundreds of them!

I shut my eyes and pushed through the curtain. I could feel their furry bodies brush my cheeks as I passed.

I shuddered. My skin itched like crazy.

I found myself in a dark hall. One flickering candle was the only light. I could hear voices in other rooms. Kids shouting and laughing. Heavy footsteps. But I couldn't see anyone else in this dark hall.

Moving slowly, I stepped into the front room. The floorboards creaked under my shoes. The whole house seemed to groan as I walked.

I heard a cat screech nearby. I glanced around the dimly lit front room. A fire smoldered in the fireplace, red embers were dying on the hearth. A human skull rested on the mantel. It turned to follow me as I walked past.

A long bloodstain ran down one wall and puddled on the carpet. A glass vase was filled with enormous eyeballs.

A woman's screams of horror rang down from somewhere above. And I heard a muffled cry: *"Help me, please. Help me, please."* A little boy's voice. It was coming from *inside* the wall!

"Awesome haunted house," I murmured. "Nice special effects."

I cried out as the window drapes suddenly flew into the room. They rose up like ghosts and brushed my face, giving me a chill, then settled down silently.

I stepped through a narrow doorway and found myself in a small den. I saw a desk in the center of the room. Tall bookshelves on the wall behind it.

The bookshelves were empty except for a small object on top. I moved closer. I squinted hard at the object. *Oh, no!* A shrunken head!

The tiny head of a man with scraggly brown hair and long buck teeth. Crooked black stitches crossed his forehead. His dark little button eyes peered out at me.

Suddenly, his dry brown lips moved. "What are you *staring* at?" he rasped.

I screamed.

The head uttered an ugly laugh.

I spun away from it, my heart pounding. Something moved. I heard a creak, then a sliding sound.

"Whoa. Wait —"

I saw the walls move. The walls were moving in on me.

"Hey!" I cried out as the ceiling dropped down. I felt a jolt. The floor was rising!

A rumbling sound. And the walls squeezed in tighter. The room grew smaller.

I climbed on top of the desk. But the ceiling came plunging down . . . lowering over me . . . sinking fast. The walls slid closer.

This was no joke. In seconds, I'd be *squeezed* to death in here!

"Hey! I'm in here!" I shouted. "Can anybody hear me? I'm here! Help! Somebody — help me!"

35

The ceiling dipped lower. The walls pressed in against the desk.

I dropped to my knees on the desktop.

I screamed again when the desk began to crack. The sliding walls were crushing it!

"Somebody — *help* me!" My cry came out muffled and shrill. "Is anybody here? I need *help* in here!"

With a groan, I raised both hands, trying to hold the ceiling off me. I pushed against it with all my strength.

The desk cracked. The walls slid in tighter.

I gave the ceiling another hard shove — and punched a large hole in it. Plaster fell all around me. I shut my eyes and waited for it to stop.

Then I gazed up at the jagged hole I had made. Was it big enough to squeeze through?

I grabbed the sides of the hole with both hands and pulled myself to my feet. I stuck my head through the hole.

Dark up there.

The ceiling dropped again. The desk was splintering under me.

I grasped the sides of the hole tightly, kicked off from the desktop, and hoisted myself up to the next floor.

"Ow!" I cried out as I scraped my arm on the jagged wood. Breathing hard, I pulled myself to my knees and rolled away from the hole.

Where was I? In a long, dark hallway. I took a few seconds to catch my breath. I could hear kids laughing somewhere far away. I heard footsteps clanging up a staircase.

I gazed around, still struggling to breathe normally. Trailing my hand along the wall, I lurched down the hallway. I had to find a way out of this creepy house.

Again, I heard a cat screech somewhere nearby. And a woman screaming in horror above my head.

I passed several rooms. The doors were all shut tight.

My shoes scraped the ragged rug as I slowly made my way through the darkness. Finally, the hallway ended. Gray light seeped up a narrow staircase. The staircase led down.

Good, I thought. *I can get back to the first floor — and out of here!*

I gripped the railing tightly and followed the

curving stairway down. The light grew brighter as I neared the bottom.

I let out a sigh of relief when I stepped back onto the first floor. I stood in a small dining room. The table was covered with an orange-and-black tablecloth. Orange candles flickered in the center.

A scowling jack-o'-lantern was placed at either end. The table was set with china dishes and covered with food platters. I saw a roasted turkey, a big ham, a bowl of mashed potatoes — and the shrunken head on a round platter.

Someone had moved it.

"Who are you, Meg?" the head demanded in a hoarse, dry whisper.

"Leave me alone!" I screamed.

"Who are you, Meg? Who are you REALLY?"

"I don't want to play this game!" I cried. "How do I get out of here?"

"Who are you *really*? And can you *prove* it?" the head croaked.

I lurched away. I let out a cry when I saw the front door ahead of me. "I made it! I'm out of here!"

I grabbed the doorknob and twisted it. I pulled.

The door didn't budge.

I tried pushing.
No.
I tried again. Again.
A cold shiver ran down the back of my neck.
Someone had locked me in.

36

I tried the doorknob again. The door still wouldn't budge.

"Hey — did somebody lock me in here?" I cried. "Can somebody let me out?"

I was panting hard. Sweat ran down my face inside the lizard mask. I had forgotten I was wearing it!

"Hey — anybody?"

Finally, I heard footsteps. Someone approaching slowly from the back hall.

The footsteps were strange. Sort of a *thud*, followed by a scraping sound.

I didn't care. Help was on the way.

"I'm trapped in here!" I called. "The door is locked."

I listened to the strange footsteps grow louder. And then a hunched figure staggered into view.

A monster. Some kind of green-headed ghoul

161

with blazing red eyes dripping with goo. A piglike nose. Scraggly hair sticking out over big pointed ears. The face was pocked and bumpy. Thick drool slid over its fat black lips and down its green chin.

"Trick or treat . . . Trick or treat . . ." the creature growled.

"That's an *awesome* costume!" I said. "Do you work here? Can you let me out?"

"Trick or treat . . . Trick or treat . . ."

He took a step closer, dragging one leg. A gob of drool hit the carpet with a *smack*. I could hear his wheezing breaths.

"Can you help me?" I asked.

"Trick or treat . . ." He raised his dripping red eyes to me and smacked his lips together. As he moved closer, I could see long dark hair sprouting from his nose.

"Do . . . do you work here?" I stammered.

"Trick or treat," he replied in a deep, ugly growl.

Something was wrong here. Very wrong.

"The door — it's locked." I tried one more time.

He began wheezing harder. Another gob of drool made a *splat* sound as it landed on his big bare feet.

"Please —" I started.

He was real. He wasn't pretending. I was staring at a *real ghoul.*

"HELP ME!" I tried to scream. But the rubber lizard mask muffled my cry.

And before I could move from the doorway, the hideous creature lowered his bulging shoulder, uttered a terrifying growl — and dove at me!

37

I ducked away.

The ghoul's hard shoulder slammed the door — and smashed it open.

He staggered forward and fell flat on his stomach.

I didn't hesitate. I took a deep breath and took off running. I jumped right over him. He growled and reached for me with both hands. He missed — and I kept running.

Sweat poured into my eyes and made it hard to see through the narrow eye slits in the lizard mask. I ran full speed. I was in a narrow alley that ran along the back of the haunted house.

No one else in view.

I could hear the shouts and laughter of park visitors on the other side of the house.

Okay. Okay. I was out. I was free! Now I just had to find a way back to the main street.

Breathing hard, I glanced back. Was the ghoul following me?

No. No sign of anyone back there.

My shoes thudded on the narrow alley pavement. All I could think of was getting back to the crowded walkway. Losing myself in the crowd. Taking a long breath. Getting a cool drink.

The alley ended at a tall brick wall. Was this a dead end? I turned at the wall and found a path to the main street.

"Oh!" I let out a startled cry as I bumped into a girl in a green costume. It took me a few seconds to recognize it. A green lizard costume.

The girl I'd seen before. The girl who had stared at me. And now, here we were, both wearing the same costume and mask.

She tilted her head as she stared back at me.

"Where did you get that lizard costume?" the girl asked me.

"The mask store," I replied. I pointed toward Zombie Plaza. "Just tonight."

"Me, too," the girl said. She had a whispery voice, like she had a cold or something.

"I saw you before," I said. "Remember? On the plaza?"

"Maybe," she replied. Staring at her mask, I realized she had green eyes like me.

My face was burning up. I had to wipe the sweat from my eyes.

I grabbed the bottom of the rubber mask,

yanked it off, and threw it on the ground. Then I mopped my face with the sleeve of my costume.

When I looked up, the other girl was pulling off her mask.

She shook out her red hair and stared back at me.

"Oh, wow!" I cried. "No. It's impossible!"

I was staring at *myself*!

38

Her mouth dropped open. She squinted hard at me in silence.

I stared back. She had my face. My long, curly red hair. My green eyes. She even had the same freckles on her nose!

She wasn't a look-alike. She was *me*!

It had to be some kind of visual trick. Some kind of special effect. A mirror image. Maybe like the 3-D holograms I saw at the art museum.

I moved closer. I couldn't resist. I reached out and brushed her cheek.

I figured she wouldn't really be there. I thought my hand would go right through her.

But no. I touched skin. She was really standing there.

She reached out and brushed back my hair. Then she jumped back, as startled and creeped out as I was!

"Who are you?" I blurted out. "I mean, what's your name?"

"I'm Meg Oliver," she replied in her whispery voice.

"No!" I cried. I raised my hands to my face. "No — you're not!"

And then it came to me. Suddenly, I caught on to what this was about.

I narrowed my eyes at her. "I get it. You're playing Chiller's game — aren't you!" I said.

She frowned at me. "Game?" She shrugged the bumpy shoulders of her lizard costume. "I don't know what you're talking about."

"Well . . . *I'm* Meg Oliver," I told her. "So you've got to be playing a game. Who are you *really*?"

"Meg Oliver," she said quietly.

I studied her face. She looked exactly like me in every way. She even had the tiny scar on my forehead I got when Chris scraped me with a sand shovel when we were little kids.

Impossible. Impossible.

"Your face is a mask — isn't it!" I cried.

"No way," she replied. "Are *you* wearing a mask?"

I grabbed for her face before she had time to grab me. I reached under her chin and searched for the bottom of the mask.

I couldn't find it.

"Hey — stop!" She squirmed out of my reach. Then she dove forward and grabbed my chin. She started to tug, twisting my head to one side.

"I'm not wearing a mask, either!" I screamed.

I lost it. I shoved her in the chest with both hands, and she fell backward. I just wanted her to let go of me. I didn't mean to push her so hard.

She stumbled back until she bumped the alley wall. Then she shook herself, like shaking off the pain. A second later, she ducked her head and came roaring at me.

She wrapped her arms around my waist and tried to tackle me to the ground.

"Let go! Let *go* of me!" I screamed, and tried to pull her arms off me. "Are you *crazy*? Let go of me!"

We wrestled standing up. She really wanted to push me to the ground. I just wanted to get her off me.

"Let go!" I pleaded.

And then I heard a familiar voice. "Hey, Meg — what's up?"

We both turned to the voice. Her hands slid off me.

I squinted at the boy running toward us down the alley.

"Chris!" I cried, staring wide-eyed at my brother. "How did *you* get here?"

39

"Meg!" he exclaimed. "That shop owner — Jonathan Chiller — he brought me here. He said something about a fun Halloween game. I —"

Chris stopped and turned to the other girl. He scrunched his face up. I could see he was confused.

"Meg, who is this girl? What's going on?"

"Chris!" I called. "You're talking to the wrong girl. This is me over here."

My brother spun around.

"That's not true," the other girl cried. "I'm the real Meg." She pointed to me. "That girl is totally crazy."

My brother's head turned from her to me, then back to her. He looked like he was watching a tennis match.

"I don't get it," he murmured. "What's this about?"

"Chris," I said, "it's part of Chiller's game." I picked my lizard mask up off the pavement. "But, game over," I said.

"Don't talk to her, Chris," the other girl said, stepping between us. "She's a total fake. I'm your sister."

"I'm your sister," I insisted. "And now that you're here, I'll win Chiller's game. You'll be able to prove to him that I'm me. Like I said, game over."

"Game over for *you*," the other girl said. She tossed her hair behind her shoulders, just the way I always do. "Now that my brother is here, I can win the game."

I glared angrily at her, breathing hard. My sides still ached from where she'd grabbed me.

I could see that poor Chris was totally confused. He was staring at identical twins. I had to find a way to show him I was his sister. I had to talk to him . . . alone.

A crowd of teenagers — at least twenty of them, all wearing scarecrow costumes — came walking by. They were some kind of high school group. I could see by the way they laughed and talked that they all knew each other.

I held my breath and waited till the scarecrows were right across from us. Then I grabbed Chris by the arm and pulled with all my strength.

I pulled him into the middle of the group, where we were hidden. I heard the other girl shouting after us. But I didn't look back.

As soon as it was safe, I tugged Chris behind a store.

Chris pulled his arm free. "What are you doing?" he demanded.

"Trying to lose her," I said. "I have to talk to you. I'm not sure exactly what's going on here. But I need you to help me win this weird game."

Chris studied me. Like he'd never seen me before. "Okay, she's gone," he said. "So?"

"So, you have to believe that I am your sister," I said.

He scrunched up his face again. "Can you prove it?" he demanded.

"Of course," I said. I grabbed his big ears and tugged them, the way I always do. "Who else would know about pulling your ears?" I asked.

He shrugged. "That doesn't really prove anything."

I let out an exasperated sigh. "Okay. Okay. I'll prove I'm the real Meg Oliver. Go ahead, Chris. Ask me anything about our life. Quiz me."

He nodded. "Okay." He thought for a few seconds. "Tell me what street we live on."

"An easy one," I said. "We live on Rosemont Avenue."

"No. That's wrong," Chris said.

40

"Huh?" I uttered a gasp. I grabbed Chris by both shoulders. "Chris, you *know* we live on Rosemont, a block away from Kelly."

He stared hard into my eyes. "Kelly?" he said. "Am I supposed to know someone named Kelly?"

"Of *course* you know Kelly," I said. "Why are you acting so weird? I don't get it, Chris."

He pushed my hands off his shoulders. "Let's try another question," he said. "One more chance."

One more chance?

The words sent a chill down my back.

Chris raised my hand. "How did you get this cut on your hand?" he asked.

"It's a paper cut," I answered. "I got it opening my science notebook. Remember?"

He shook his head. "No. That's not right," he said. "I was there. Meg cut her hand slicing an apple."

"*I'm* Meg!" I screamed. "I'm telling the truth! Why are you doing this? Why are you lying?"

I tried to grab him again. I wanted to pull his ears hard. Or shake him till he told the truth.

But he took a step back. His eyes burned into mine. "*You're* lying," he said softly. "You're not my real sister. You couldn't answer one question."

"Okay, Chris, what about this week? Bim? The crazy Weirdo? And the Floig?"

"Are you making those words up?" he asked. "I don't know what you're talking about."

"Ohhh!" I let out a cry. "You liar! You *liar*!"

Then suddenly I realized what was happening.

"Chiller told you to lie — didn't he!" I cried. "I get it. This is part of his game."

Chris didn't answer. He stood staring at me with his eyes narrowed, as if he was thinking hard.

"Tell me!" I shouted. "He told you what to say — didn't he! You are playing his game, too."

"You've already lost," Chris said. "Whoever you are — you've already lost."

"No!" I cried. "No!"

But he spun away from me and took off into the crowd. I watched him push his way through a group of kids. Then he lowered his head and ran hard back toward the haunted house.

"Chris — please!" I shouted. I started after him. But a food cart rolled in front of me, and I nearly ran right into it.

When I caught my balance, I couldn't see him.

"Chris!" I shouted. "Come back! I have to win this game! We have to go home!"

My voice cracked. People turned to stare at me. But I didn't care.

I ran after him, screaming. "Chris — please! You're my only hope!"

41

I lost Chris for a moment. Then I saw him running along the high wall behind the haunted house.

I didn't see the other girl in the lizard costume, the girl pretending to be me. Was Chris running to her?

I called to my brother again and again. But my cries were drowned out by the shouts and laughter of trick-or-treaters.

I saw Chris turn a corner and head down a crowded road. Then a big costumed Horror stepped in my way.

I tried to dodge around him. But I had to stop and stare. His head . . . his head was a big jack-o'-lantern. And flames danced behind the cut-out eyes and mouth. Fire from *inside his head*!

People gathered around him, oohing and ahhing. How did he do it?

To my shock, he turned his flaming head to

me. "Who are you?" he cried. Flames shot out of his jagged mouth with each word. "Who are you *really*?"

I backed away from him. "I know who I am!" I shouted.

"What if you're WRONG?" His words were a hiss of fire.

I swerved around him and cut through the crowd. I searched in one direction, then the other. And I saw Chris.

He was running through a doorway jammed with kids. A big orange neon sign above the door read: THE HALLOWEEN HOPPER.

I was panting hard by the time I reached the door. I cut through the crowd and entered.

"Whoa." An enormous trampoline filled the large room. The trampoline was as big as my living room! Kids were leaping and bouncing, tumbling and laughing.

Music blared all around. I couldn't make out the words to the song. Something like, "Hop hop hop. Do the hop hop hop . . ."

Some kids were bouncing in time to the music. Others were trying to leap as high as they could. It was so crowded, kids fell and bounced into each other.

I saw Chris climb onto the trampoline. He moved toward the center and started to jump.

Why was he doing this?

I couldn't guess.

But I grabbed the edge of the trampoline. And hoisted myself onto the net.

I lost my balance. Landed headfirst — and rolled into two kids wearing monster costumes. They went tumbling to the net.

I thought they might be angry. But they just laughed.

I climbed to my feet and struggled to stand as the net bounced beneath me. It took a while to get the rhythm. But soon I was bouncing with everyone else.

As I bounced, I searched for Chris. Finally, I spotted him jumping next to a girl in a princess costume and a Harry Potter look-alike. The girl was holding her tiara down on her head as she jumped. She kept bumping into Chris, nearly knocking him over.

"Chris!" I shouted as I jumped. "We have to talk!"

He couldn't hear me.

I tried to edge closer. I had to get to him. I had to convince him that I was his real sister. But the trampoline was too jammed with kids. I couldn't move.

Suddenly, I heard a loud buzz, like an engine starting up. I felt a powerful vibration beneath my feet.

Kids screamed as they began to bounce harder.

My feet hit the net and I felt myself shoot into

the air. Another jump, and the vibrating net sent me flying even higher.

Higher. Harder. The black starry sky came down to meet me. It was almost like flying.

It would have been fun to jump so high. Except that I felt totally out of control. I couldn't stop jumping. I couldn't move off the net. Couldn't get to Chris.

Faster. The trampoline began to whip us up and down, tossing us high into the air.

Kids screamed. A few jumped off the edge and tumbled onto the ground.

"Somebody stop this thing!" I shouted. My legs ached with each jump. My knees throbbed. I couldn't catch my breath.

The buzz grew louder, and the trampoline whipped us higher.

I'm going to break my neck! I thought.

I looked for Chris. I saw him jumping next to a girl in a green costume. The girl who claimed to be me.

"Chris!" I shouted. "Chris!" And then my knees gave way. I fell on top of some costumed kids.

"Oof!" I landed hard on my back. My breath shot out in a *whoosh*.

My chest flared with pain. I struggled to breathe. I was choking, sputtering.

The trampoline tossed me up again.

As I came down, I heard a deafening *POP*.

I landed on my back. The net gave way beneath me.

I tensed my muscles, waiting to be shot up high again.

But no. The net sank beneath me. I could feel it collapsing.

I heard a loud *hiss*. Like air going out of a balloon.

The trampoline net collapsed in on itself. I sank to the ground in a heap.

All around me, kids were scrambling to their feet. Everyone was stampeding out of The Halloween Hopper. Some costumes were torn. Masks were left in the net.

I gripped my mask in one hand and straightened the lizard costume over me. Sweat poured down my forehead. I pushed my hair out of my eyes and searched for my brother.

"Chris? Hey — Chris?"

Peering into the crowd of kids, I spotted him on the other side of the trampoline. He was making his way out a back exit. Walking with the other girl in the lizard costume.

Had he made up his mind? Did he really think she was me? How could I prove to him that he was wrong?

My head spun with questions. If only I could get to him. If only he would *listen* to me.

I'm his sister, I thought. *Why isn't he on my side?*

180

42

Chris and the other girl were walking fast, moving quickly through the crowd. I stepped out of the exit. Most kids were hurrying along the side of The Halloween Hopper on their way back to the main street.

But Chris and the girl didn't follow them. They turned left and disappeared into the darkness.

"Chris?" I shouted. I started to run after him. I found myself in another dark and narrow alley. Wooden fences rose up on both sides. My shoes scraped the gravel as I ran to catch up to my brother.

A pale glimmer of moonlight fell over the alley. I could see the two of them up ahead, walking fast.

I started to jog. "Hey — stop!" I called. "Stop!"

I knew they could hear me. But they kept walking. Again, they disappeared into total darkness.

I turned a corner. I saw them again. Chris glanced back. He saw me. But he kept walking.

I knew what they were doing. They were leading me down this dark alley. Leading me *where*?

Another sharp turn. And I suddenly blinked into bright light. A bonfire.

Tall flames licked the black sky. Blown by the wind, red embers floated up from the fire.

I could hear the crackling of the fire over the low chanting of the people who circled it. People dancing in slow motion around the tall bonfire.

I took a few steps closer. Close enough to feel the heat of the flames on my face.

And as I drew near, I had to stop again. And stare at the ugly decomposing faces, the empty eye sockets, the missing arms and legs, the skeletal, grinning faces.

Zombies!

I realized I was holding my breath. I let it out in a long *whoosh*.

I had to remind myself this was Halloween.

These zombies weren't real. They weren't humans back from the dead. They were people in costumes.

But why were they all dressed as zombies? And why were they chanting and dancing so slowly around this crackling, blazing fire?

They uttered moans and groans as they danced

in their circle. They moved so stiffly, as if their arms and legs wouldn't bend.

I gazed past the fire. I thought I saw Chris on the other side. I didn't see the other girl.

I started to make my way around the fire toward Chris. But one of the costumed zombies caught my eye.

She stopped her dance and turned to look at me. Her whole face was nearly eaten away. Just a few chunks of flesh left on her forehead and cheeks.

She grinned at me. Such an ugly, skeletal grin.

She had something in her hand. She raised it to me. Her sleeves were ragged and torn and stained with dirt.

I stared at the object in her hand. Stepped closer. Unable to take my eyes off it.

She held it out to me. She moved it up and down so I could see it clearly.

"No!" A scream escaped my throat. "No! It can't be! No way!"

It was a rag doll. A voodoo doll. *And it looked exactly like ME!*

As I stared in shock, the zombie woman raised the doll high — and tossed it into the flames.

43

"Nooooo!" A scream of horror burst from my throat.

I didn't think. I just dove forward. Into the flames. Shot my hand into the fire — and yanked out the doll.

Its hair smoked and sizzled. A single flame flickered on its back.

I hugged it to me. Pressed it against the front of my T-shirt.

I felt a stab of heat. The flame died quickly. The smoke sizzled out.

I held the doll in both hands. I saved it from burning. Did I also save *myself*?

The zombies continued their slow, stiff dance. They chanted in low voices as they circled the fire. Their faces were red and charred, as if they'd stepped too close to the flames.

Madame Doom!

That strange fortune-teller flashed into my mind from my first visit to HorrorLand. And I pictured the voodoo doll she handed me. The rag doll that looked *exactly like me*!

Was it the same voodoo doll that Madame Doom had handed me? Did Madame Doom know that I'd be returning to HorrorLand? Did she know about Jonathan Chiller?

Beyond the crackling fire, I saw a figure move down the alley. Chris!

I took a deep breath and forced my trembling legs to move. I had to talk to him. Why was he leading me on such a long, frightening chase?

"Chris! Hey — Chris! Give me a break! Wait up!"

I followed him into a crowded street. I saw where he was heading. Toward a small hamburger restaurant called The Slurp 'n' Burp. A loudspeaker on the restaurant roof sent out long, disgusting burps.

Not very appetizing.

A girl stepped out of the restaurant. The girl who looked exactly like me. She held her lizard mask in one hand and rested her other hand against the storefront.

"There you are, Meg," I heard Chris call to her. "I lost you at the zombie bonfire!"

"Noooo!" A shout burst from my throat. My heart started to pound in my chest.

I held my breath as I watched them from a distance. Chiller said he wouldn't send me home until I proved I was me. If Chris decided the other girl was Meg, how would I ever get home?

I suddenly realized I was in even worse trouble. Chiller never told me what would happen if I *lost* his game!

Chris isn't going to help me, I told myself. *For some reason, he's trying to make me lose. I've got to get out of here on my own.*

My hand trembled as I reached under the costume and grabbed my cell phone. I had to try to call my parents one more time. Maybe Chiller wouldn't be there this time.

I watched Chris and the other girl talking at the side of the restaurant. The long burps from the loudspeaker were sickening. I pressed a finger into one ear, punched in my dad's number, and raised the phone to my other ear.

Please be there. Please . . .

The phone rang twice. Then a voice said, "Aren't you enjoying my game?"

Jonathan Chiller.

"No. No, I'm not!" I cried. My voice cracked on the words. "I don't like this game. I . . . I want to go home!"

Silence for a moment. Then Chiller said softly, "You're making me sad. Very sad. I made up the game especially for you."

"It's not a game!" I cried. "I don't understand it. It doesn't make any sense! I . . . don't stand a chance. I —"

"Keep trying," Chiller said. "You're a clever girl. I know you can win."

"I don't care," I started. "Listen to me —"

"If you win, I promise I won't keep you," Chiller said. "I won't keep you or your brother here in HorrorLand one minute longer."

"But that's the problem," I said. "My brother is acting weird. He —"

I heard a click. "Are you there?" I cried. "Are you still there?"

No. The line was dead.

I let out an angry cry. I stared at the phone in my hand.

And suddenly I realized I had *won*!

44

I gazed at my phone. A smile crossed my face.

How could I prove to Jonathan Chiller I was Meg Oliver?

Simple. My cell phone would prove it. My phone has all my contacts in it. That's as good as an I.D.

I'd won the game. Now I just had to let everyone know it.

I wanted to tell Chris and the other girl that the game was over. But I didn't see them in front of The Slurp 'n' Burp anymore.

They must have wandered away while I was on the phone with Chiller.

Okay. No problem. I'd catch up with them later.

I suddenly felt so much better. So much calmer and happier.

I heaved the lizard mask into the air. I left it on the ground where it fell. I pulled off the green costume, crinkled it into a ball, and tossed it into a trash can. Then I smoothed down my jeans and shirt.

A group of laughing kids came out of the restaurant. I felt like laughing, too.

I knew I had won. I had beat Chiller at his own game.

The kids took turns burping really loud along with the loudspeaker burps. They thought it was a riot.

I raised my phone and punched REDIAL. I knew Chiller would pick up again. I couldn't wait to tell him how I'd won. How I could prove that I'm me.

The phone rang twice.

"Hi, it's me again," I said.

"Who is this?" a girl's voice demanded. I recognized the whispery voice. The other girl!

"Get off!" I cried. "Get off the phone!"

"This is Meg Oliver," she said. "Who are you? Who are you *really*?"

45

"NOOOO! GET OFFFFF!"

I shrieked into the phone at the top of my voice.

"Sorry. You have the wrong number," the girl said. "This is Meg Oliver."

"No. No way." My heart pounding, I clicked the phone shut. Then I opened it again and pushed CONTACTS.

No. Oh, no. This couldn't be happening.

My contacts were gone. The whole list was erased.

How could that be? It was my only way to win the game.

I saw Chris and the girl across the way. They were following a crowd of costumed kids.

I didn't plan to let them get away. I wanted to end the game — now.

I shouted Chris's name and bolted after them. Running hard, I tripped over a baby stroller. The mother screamed angrily at me as I kept going.

Chris and the other Meg were disappearing into a huge black building. The sign above the entrance read: WORLD'S MOST DANGEROUS PUMPKIN PIE!

Pushing kids out of my way, I hurtled in after the two of them. I glanced around. The building was as big as a hockey arena.

Everyone was walking on a catwalk high above the floor. And far down below, I saw an *enormous* pumpkin pie. The pie was as big as our town swimming pool! I mean, it was *gigantic*!

The crust around the pie was at least six feet high. The pumpkin filling was smooth and shiny under the rafter lights. It had to be filled with *hundreds* of gallons of pumpkin!

I didn't have time to think about it. I ran along the narrow catwalk, holding on to the metal rail. The catwalk swayed from side to side as I ran.

People on the catwalk were screaming and laughing as it swung hard beneath them. Everyone gripped the handrail tightly. One slip — and you could plunge down into the pie.

Struggling to balance on the narrow walk, I pushed my way up to the fake Meg. "Why are you doing this?" I cried angrily. "Admit it! Admit it to Chris that you're not the real Meg Oliver!"

"*You're* not!" she screamed. Her green eyes flashed. "You're not! *You're* not!"

"I'm Meg!" I cried. "I'm Meg!"

I bumped her hard. I didn't mean to. Someone pushed me from behind.

She let out a low growl — and pushed me back with both hands.

I stumbled against the rail. The narrow catwalk swayed. The catwalk floor tilted up beneath me.

I grabbed on to her to keep from tumbling off.

She must have thought I was trying to fight. With another growl, she pushed me again.

My hands flew into the air.

I screamed as I fell backward.

I hit the rail hard. Bounced forward. Grabbed her by the waist, trying to stay on the catwalk.

She staggered back. Back . . .

And we went sailing over the edge.

We both screamed all the way down.

46

I landed with a heavy *splaaaaat* on top of the pie. I heard the other Meg splash down beside me.

I hit so hard, it took my breath away. Struggling against the pain in my chest, I felt myself sink into the gooey pumpkin filling.

I slapped my hands against the surface, trying to keep my head over the goo. But my hands plunged into the goo. My whole body was sinking fast.

I kicked my feet. Then I tried to stand. But where was the bottom?

The pie was so deep.

I heard the other Meg shrieking and calling for help. I heard her slapping at the surface of the pie filling.

The sticky orange goo rose over me like an ocean wave. Thick and wet, it was pulling me down . . . pulling me . . .

Like quicksand! I thought.

My shoulders sank beneath the heavy, wet pumpkin. I raised my arms high and struggled to climb up.

But no. Every move I made caused me to sink faster.

I tried to swim to the top. But the filling was too thick.

In seconds, I knew I would sink.

I heard the other Meg screaming for help.

And from up above, I heard people cheering and laughing. The people up on the catwalk were enjoying the show! Couldn't they see we were in real trouble down here?

I raised my eyes and saw something move above me. I squinted up at it. A red-and-white can.

The shadow of the can swept over me. Its top tilted down toward the pie. It took me a few seconds to read the label on its side: WHIPPED CREAM.

A gigantic spray can of whipped cream!

No — please! I thought.

The can slid across the ceiling with a loud hum. It moved over the center of the pumpkin pie.

Splaaaash.

A heavy blob of whipped cream crashed onto the pie. The crowd cheered.

I screamed. It missed me by only a few inches.

"Stop it! Somebody turn it off!" Was that *me* screeching in total panic?

Splaaaash.

Everything went black as a thick layer of whipped cream covered me. The heavy cream stuck to my head, covered my eyes, my nose. Covered me . . . and pushed me deeper into the pie filling.

"Stop it! *Stop* it!"

I heard the crowd let out another wild cheer as a third *splat* shot out of the enormous can. It hit my head hard.

I took a deep breath and held it as my head plunged under the surface.

I stretched my toes down, trying to touch the bottom. But the pie was too deep.

I couldn't see. Couldn't move. I tried frantically to shove the whipped cream off me. But it was too thick and sticky.

My chest felt about to burst. I couldn't hold my breath any longer.

One more try, I thought. *I have to make one more try to pull myself out of this.*

But I didn't have the strength.

47

Don't give up, Meg. You can do this.

I gritted my teeth and forced my arms up. Carefully, I raised myself onto my back. I spread my arms wide and tried to stay very still and float on the top.

And then I saw something big and white bouncing over the pie. At first, I thought it was a boat. A rescue team floating across the pie to drag us out.

As it came closer, I could see its shape. It was a pie cutter. A huge white plastic pie cutter.

It floated closer. I waited . . . waited. And then I reached up and grabbed on to it.

My hands were slippery, covered in orange goo. But I held on tight. I shut my eyes and hoped it would carry me out of the pie.

I heard a voice. I turned and saw the other Meg grasping the other side. Her hair, her face, her clothes were all covered in pumpkin chunks and whipped cream.

The giant pie cutter swung us to the crust at the side of the pie. We both toppled over the side and dropped onto the floor. I fell onto my back . . . rolled away from the pie. My feet kept slipping in goo as I struggled to my feet.

I brushed orange pumpkin off my face. I knew I'd never forget the feeling of almost drowning in a pumpkin pie. And I'd never forget the *smell*.

When I looked up, the other Meg was staring at me with a scowl on her face. "Copycat," she muttered.

The next few minutes were an orange blur. Two Horrors led us to a shower room. I took a long, hot shower.

It took several shampoos to get the pumpkin gunk out of my hair. And even longer to get the smell off my skin.

When I came out, my jeans and top had been cleaned and dried.

"I almost *drowned* in there," I told the Horror taking care of me.

"What a delicious way to go!" she replied.

I stared at her. Had I really been in danger? Or was this another HorrorLand trick?

I didn't want to think about it.

When I stepped out of the pie building, Chris and the other Meg were waiting for me. "You look good in orange," she sneered. "It's your color."

I turned to my brother. "See? Doesn't that prove to you that *I'm* the real Meg? I'm *never* mean like that!"

Chris rolled his eyes. "Just follow me," he said. He turned and started striding quickly through the crowded street.

"Where are we going?" I asked. I had to trot to catch up.

"We have to settle this," Chris replied.

Settle this?

We crossed Zombie Plaza. I felt a chill as we passed the Madame Doom fortune-telling booth. The wooden figure sat stiffly in her glass booth. The picture of that voodoo rag doll flashed again in my mind.

I knew where Chris was leading us. I saw the little souvenir shop up ahead and the sign over the front door: CHILLER HOUSE.

Jonathan Chiller pulled open the door and motioned us inside. He peered through his square glasses at the other Meg, then at me. A smile spread slowly over his wrinkled face.

Before I could say anything, the other Meg spoke up:

"I'm tired of this game. I really hate it. I just want to go home."

"Whoa. Stop!" I cried. "*I* want to go home. I'm the one who was dragged here to play this crazy game."

"You're not fooling anyone," the other girl snapped. "Why don't you just give up?"

Chris turned from her to me. His face was a blank. I couldn't tell what he was thinking.

"Stop this! *Stop* this!" I cried. I grabbed Chris by the shoulders. "Tell Chiller who I am! Go ahead — tell him!"

Chiller raised a hand and motioned for me to calm down. "Maybe we can end this game happily," he said softly.

I let go of Chris. He took a step away from me.

My heart was pounding. I could feel the blood pulsing at my temples.

This whole thing was *crazy*! I was frantic to end the game — and *win*!

Chiller turned to Chris. "You're the brother. You know everything." He pointed to the other Meg. "Ask her some questions," Chiller said.

Chris nodded. He turned to the other girl. "What street do you and I live on?" he asked.

The other girl didn't hesitate. "Rosemont Avenue," she said.

"That's right," Chris said.

"Wait a minute!" I cried. "That's too easy." I glared at Chris. "Before, you said it wasn't the right answer. Why did you lie before?"

Chris didn't answer me. He looked over my shoulder at Chiller.

"Be patient," Chiller said to me. "You'll have your turn."

Chris turned back to the phony Meg. "Who is your Spanish teacher?" he asked.

Again, the other girl didn't hesitate. "Mrs. Smith," she answered.

"That's right," Chris said.

I stared at her. At her red hair and green eyes and freckled nose. How did she know all these details about my life?

"I'll ask her a question," I said. "Okay if I ask one?"

"Go ahead," Chiller said.

"*No way* she knows the answer to this one," I said. I turned to her. "What nickname did my dad call me when I was little?"

Her mouth dropped open. "Nickname?"

48

"See?" I cried. "That proves it! She's a fake!"

"Nutmeg," the other girl said. "Dad called me Nutmeg."

I gasped. My legs suddenly felt weak. It took me a moment to catch my breath.

"How . . . how did you know that?" I stammered.

"Because she's the real Meg," Chris said.

She tossed back her red hair and flashed me a sick smile. "Why wouldn't I know what my dad called me when I was little?"

"Because he called ME Nutmeg!" I screamed.

And then I couldn't help it. I totally lost it.

I grabbed a skull candle from the shelf next to me and heaved it against the wall. I grabbed a handful of Monster Sour Gummis and tossed them at the ceiling.

"Stop! Please — stop!" Jonathan Chiller cried. He pressed his hands over his ears.

I didn't even realize I'd been screaming.

But I was too furious to stop myself.

"Chris — you're my brother!" I cried. "How can you be on *her* side?"

And then I stormed up to him. I grabbed him by his big ears.

I tugged hard —

— and opened my mouth in a shriek of horror as his ears *came off in my hands!*

49

My hands trembled as I stared down at them. Stared down at the rubbery ears I had pulled off Chris.

Only it wasn't Chris. It couldn't be Chris.

He had two holes in the sides of his head. And inside the holes I saw wires and gears, computer chips and metal springs.

"You're not Chris!" I shouted. "You're a stupid *robot*!"

It was all a game — and it was rigged against me.

Was the fake Meg a robot, too? Of course. She *had* to be!

Jonathan Chiller dreamed the whole thing up. Just to frighten me. Just because he loved to play scary games.

I didn't care. I knew the truth now.

I tossed the ears at Chris. They bounced off his chest.

Then I stuck my hands in his ear holes and started to twist his head. "Game over! Game over!" I screamed.

"Stop!" I heard Jonathan Chiller's cry behind me.

I turned my eyes toward him. But I kept my hands tightly on the robot's head.

"Let go! Don't break him!" Chiller cried. "He cost a *fortune*!"

I pointed at the other Meg. She had frozen stiffly by the counter. Her eyes were blank and glassy.

"She's a robot, too — *isn't* she!" I shouted at Chiller.

He nodded. "Yes," he said. "You win. The game is over. Please, Meg — let go of the Chris robot. Don't damage him."

The Chris robot struggled to pull free. I could hear circuits popping inside his head. I held on tightly to the ear holes.

"How did you do it?" I asked Chiller. "Tell me. How did you give her my memory?"

He shrugged. "It's easy," he said softly.

"What do you mean?" I demanded.

"Memory cells are easy to scan," Chiller explained. He pointed to the front entrance. "See that machine you walk through when you enter the store?"

"Yes. It looks like a metal detector," I said. "Like they have at airports."

"It isn't a metal detector," Chiller said. "It's a very special scanner I designed. It scans everyone's total memory. And their DNA."

That's impossible! I thought.

But no. I'd seen it with my own eyes. The Meg robot had my memory. And she had my looks, every detail.

"Why did you build these robots?" I asked him.

"For my special doll collection," Chiller replied. "You collect dolls, too, Meg. That's why I thought you'd be perfect for my Halloween game here in the park."

His shoulders sagged. His face went pale. He suddenly looked much older.

"I had a lonely childhood," he said softly. "I spent day after day in my room, inventing games for myself. Now I like to share my games with others. I'm sorry if you didn't enjoy it."

"Just send me home," I said. "You promised."

I still had hold of the robot Chris's head. I gave it a twist. It made a *pinging* sound.

"Please — let go of it!" Chiller begged. "The game is over. You won, Meg. It's over. I promise."

I let out a sigh of relief. I relaxed my hold on the robot, and it fell back against the wall.

"Are you going to send me home?" I asked.

Chiller walked to the front of the shop. He pushed a button on the counter.

"Hey!" I cried out in surprise as a deafening alarm rang out over the store.

A second later, the front door swung open.

The door crashed against the wall. And two big Horrors in orange-and-black guard uniforms burst into the store. They lumbered up to Chiller. Their beefy hands were wrapped around metal clubs at their waists.

"These are the Robot Guards," Chiller announced.

They both nodded. They were tall and broad and mean looking. One of them had a furry yellow mustache. He pulled his black cap lower over his forehead and glared at the three of us.

"Shall we take the robots to the reprogrammer?" he asked in a gruff growl.

"Yes, I'm done with these two robots," Chiller told them. "Take them away and change their faces. And don't forget to erase their memories."

Thank goodness, I thought. *The game really is over.*

The mustached guard grabbed the Chris robot by the waist and lifted it off the floor. "What happened to its ears?" he asked.

"They came off," Chiller replied. "These things aren't as well built as I thought."

Shaking his head, Chiller turned and headed toward the back of the shop. "Be right back, Meg," he said. "I have to get something for you."

The Chris robot slumped lifelessly in the guard's arms. The big Horror started to carry him away.

The other guard moved quickly toward the Meg robot and me. To my shock, he grabbed *me* around the waist with one arm and hoisted *me* off the floor.

At first, I was too startled to speak.

He tightened his grip and carried me toward the door.

"Let go! Let *go* of me!" I finally found my voice.

"You're making a mistake!" I screamed. "I'm not the robot. *She* is!"

The Horror acted as if he didn't hear me.

I twisted my body and kicked my legs. I tried to bite him. I tried to hit him.

But he was too strong for me.

He kept his eyes straight ahead and tightened his arm around me.

"Sometimes they don't like to be reprogrammed," he told his partner.

"Let go! Let go! I'm *not* the robot!" I shrieked.

But he began to take longer strides as he carried me to the door. "Don't fight," he said softly. "It doesn't hurt to have your brain wiped."

50

We were nearly to the door. I turned back and saw the Meg robot standing in the aisle. She didn't speak or move. Her green eyes were locked on me.

"Mr. Chiller!" I screamed. "Help me! Help! Mr. Chiller! Where are you?"

Yellow light poured out from the supply closet on the back wall. But he didn't come back out.

"Mr. Chiller — *please!*"

Chiller had no way of knowing the mistake the Horror was making. If he didn't come out of that supply closet, it would be too late for me.

My brain would be wiped clean.

"Mr. Chiller! Can't you hear me?"

The powerful Horror hoisted me higher off the floor. He bounced as he walked. He paid no attention to my screams or my kicking and thrashing.

I had to save myself. But — how?

I had to prove to this Horror that I wasn't a robot.

We were at the front of the store. About to pass the last display shelf.

I saw something on the shelf. It gave me a wild idea.

I grabbed for it. Missed. Grabbed again.

And pulled it into my hand.

I remembered seeing it before. King Kong's Diaper Pin. It was a gigantic safety pin, nearly three feet long.

As the Horror stepped up beside his partner carrying the Chris robot, I pried open the huge pin.

I waited until we were right next to the other Horror. Then I plunged the pin deep into Chris's neck.

51

The Horrors stopped. They stared at Chris. They stared at the silvery pin jabbed deep in his neck.

Of course, the robot didn't scream or move.

I pulled the giant pin out of Chris's neck.

Both guards narrowed their eyes at me. I had their attention now.

I took a deep breath and held it.

Then I scraped the pin along the cut on my hand.

The Horrors stared as red blood began to seep from the open cut.

"This one is *human*!" the mustached guard cried.

My guard uttered a low groan. "Whoa. We made a mistake."

He lowered me carefully to the floor. He eyed me from head to foot. "No harm done," he said.

He pulled a handkerchief from his uniform

pocket and helped me wrap it around my cut. Then he led the way back to Jonathan Chiller.

Chiller came walking out of the supply closet. He was standing at the front counter.

I watched him hand a tiny Horror doll to the robot Meg. His eyes went wide in surprise as the guards brought me back to him.

"We made a small mistake," my guard said. "Wrong girl."

Chiller gasped. He squinted at the handkerchief wrapped around my hand. "I'm sorry, Meg," he said to me. His face turned bright red. "I'm so embarrassed."

"You're *embarrassed*?" I cried. "I could have had my brain erased!"

"But you won the game after all, Meg," Chiller said. "I'm proud of you."

"I just want to go home now," I told him.

Chiller nodded. "I'll send you home safe and sound," he said. "Just as I promised."

He placed the little Horror in my hands. "I went back to the supply closet to get this little guy," he said. "Just wrap your hands around it and shut your eyes."

Was this some kind of a trick?

I had no reason to trust him.

But I had no choice.

I did as he said. I wrapped the tiny Horror between my fingers and squeezed it tightly. And I shut my eyes.

Nothing happened.

Nothing.

And then I suddenly felt dizzy. As if I couldn't stand up straight.

I felt a cold wave wash over me. The floor felt soft and quivery.

I bent my knees and tilted from side to side as the floor started to rock.

Was he really sending me home?

Wave after wave washed over me. I felt as if I were falling through them . . . falling through the sky.

Then it all stopped. I stood perfectly still, listening to the silence.

I opened my eyes. And gazed into a white blur.

A solid white blur.

Chiller *lied*!

Where did he send me?

52

I shook my head hard. Slowly, the whiteness faded away.

I blinked. Once. Twice. My vision came back.

I was standing in my bedroom. Staring at the empty shelves where my doll collection had been.

"YAAAAY!" I let out a long, happy cry.

I was home! Home!

I went tearing down the stairs. I burst into the kitchen.

Penny was at the sink, making a cup of tea. Her face filled with surprise as I came flying into the room.

I wrapped my arms around her and hugged her tightly. "I'm back!" I cried. "Did you miss me? Were you worried?"

Penny's mouth dropped open. "Miss you?"

She squinted at me. "Meg, you're joking — right? You were only up in your room for ten minutes."

"Huh?" I uttered a gasp. "Ten minutes?"

She nodded.

I forced a laugh. "Yeah. Just kidding," I said. "See you later."

I ran back upstairs. I was *desperate* to tell Chris what had happened to me.

But I stopped at the doorway to my room and peered inside.

I saw someone sitting on my bed. "Hey —" I called.

She sat up as I strode in. *The other Meg!*

She jumped to her feet and put her hands on her waist. Then she scowled at me.

"What are YOU doing here?" she cried angrily. "How did you get in my room?"

MADAME DOOM

REAL NAME: Ms. Doom

HOMETOWN: Europe

OCCUPATION: Fortune-teller, card reader, liar

PROUDEST ACHIEVEMENT:
"I predicted my own birth."

HORRORLAND SPLAT STATS

FORTUNES TOLD:	● ● ● ● ● ○ ○ ○ ○ ○
FORTUNES LOST:	● ● ● ● ● ● ● ● ○ ○
CRYSTAL BALLS SAT ON:	● ● ● ● ● ● ● ● ● ●
TURBAN SIZE:	● ● ● ● ● ● ● ○ ○ ○
TOTAL CREEPINESS:	● ● ● ● ● ● ● ● ● ●

Madame Doom can see your future and it doesn't look good. She predicts you will lose a lot of money. Why? Because she just stole your wallet. Madame Doom also predicts: "Tomorrow will come soon." If you say that's a dumb prediction, she says, "I predicted you'd say that."